The Sunshine Room

To Cathy—
always bring your
own sunshine. and
remember, the ficus understands.

Jan Stafford Kellis

Myrno Moss Perspectives

Jan Kellis

09.2016

Other Books by Jan Stafford Kellis

Fiction

Superior Sacrifices

The Word That You Heard

Non-Fiction

Bookworms Anonymous, Volumes I and II

A Pocketful of Light: 13 Days In The World's First Tourist Destination

This is for my daughters, Dani & Steph.

I'll never leave you, even if
you eat sugar and butter sandwiches and stop combing your hair.
But please, don't do those things.

Love, Mom

Alphabet Poem

As the saying goes, "We'll see."
By that I mean
Children, and how they turn out;
DNA notwithstanding, mine are
Exemplary specimens.
Fiercely independent women,
Girls grown too fast, impossible now to
Hold tight by the hand.
Imagine a child, born empty, filled with dreams in the
January of her life.
Killing time, desperately
Losing childhood, shedding experience like last year's
Miniskirt as useless, trivial ephemera;
Nearing adulthood at warp speed, ever
Observant of biological maturities, embracing
Puberty in its wildest form.
Quickly, carelessly forging ahead to discover everything is
Relevant, for all that came before conspired to produce this reality.
Sacrificing youth to the age-old irony, appreciating post-loss the
Tribulations endured, the clichéd experience gained.

Under-funded, under-prepared by the headlong rush into
Victorious, rule-free adulthood only to learn Mom was right!
We *do* have rules to follow; there *is* no free lunch, no map; the term
Xenon *does* come up in conversation (albeit rarely),
Youth is wasted on the young, and one must approach life with
Zeal every day.

--Jan Kellis

Elle: March 31, 2008

They say there are three sides to every story: his, hers, and the truth. In my case, there were four sides: his, hers, mine, and the truth.

Like most stories, it began before we knew we were acting out events worth retelling. Well. Some of us may have known.

As far back as I can remember, I wanted a do-over. I daydreamed about it, obsessed about it, watched and re-watched *Back To The Future* and wished I had a DeLorean and access to plutonium.

A do-over would have given me the option to really invent myself, to fulfill my greatest potential. Who knows what I could have been: a lawyer, an architect, an engineer. I could have influenced the world.

January 5, 1985

She'd been up for hours wandering the house, making coffee and drinking too much of it. The moon, she was certain, was to blame for her restlessness. The knock on the door startled her. She tugged on the belt of her ancient terrycloth robe and approached the door.

She peered through the dusty window next to the door but it only afforded a view of the top of a down-turned head. Something familiar about it. A thin thread of foreboding uncoiled in her stomach and threatened to choke her. How had he found her? Why hadn't he stopped searching?

She considered running, sprinting out the back door, one child tucked under each arm, but she knew it was futile to attempt an escape. He'd found her here, in her safe haven. A place she hadn't known existed when she'd last seen him.

She opened the door.

"Sam." She pulled back and swallowed vomit before it spewed onto his shoes.

"I've missed you, sweetness." His sneer was terrifying—it signaled the beginning of a particularly brutal attack—but she remembered the best course of action was not to show her fear.

She shoved her hand into her robe and removed her wedding ring as she talked. "No, no. I thought you wanted me to leave. Honest. I left because I thought it was what you wanted."

"You never could lie, could you, Beth. In fact—"

He leaned close as if to nuzzle her neck, and she flinched back two steps.

"—I always considered your inability to lie one of your best character flaws."

"Lie, truth, whatever. I'm stating facts." She blinked, a caricature of honesty.

"Car's running." He jabbed a thumb over his shoulder toward the street.

More bile. She held up her hands, showed him double stop signs. "I can't leave."

"Pack. Your. Bags."

She shook her head. "No. I—"

"So we'll travel light." He grabbed her wrist.

"Okay, okay." How to stall? "Give me a few minutes." She'd run into the girls' room and grab her babies, then jump out the window and run as fast as she could. It was crazy, but no way she'd leave without her babies. What could she do? She had no choice. She knew she couldn't take the babies with her—Sam wouldn't hesitate to sell them off, and they'd be safe here. Their father could raise them. He'd do a good job.

"Go ahead. Try to escape again. I know you've got a couple of marketable little princesses in the other room, and I'm not opposed to selling them off to the highest bidder." He laughed cruelly. "Or the first bidder."

"You wouldn't!"

He spoke deliberately. "I would, and you know I would. Now pack your bags. Your little mister will figure things out. He'll get by without you, don't you worry about him. And if you get your perky little ass in gear in the next ten minutes, he won't have to know about your past." He smiled, an evil snake's smile with glassy eyes and pointy chin. "You haven't told him about your past, have you?"

"Well, I—"

"No, you haven't. Or he wouldn't have married you and given you two valuable babies."

"You stop it right now."

"I'll stop. If you pack. Your. Bags. I'm getting tired of waiting. Beth."

She couldn't stomach the thought of her

husband finding out about her past. She'd been so careful to cover her tracks. How had Sam found her hundreds of miles from where she'd left him?

She ran into the bedroom to pack her things. She threw on a pair of jeans and a shirt, then scrawled a note on the index card she'd been using as a bookmark. She shoved the note into her jewelry box, where it stuck in the lid. Perfect. She scrawled a second note, a decoy in case Sam came in here, and left it on the bed.

Beth crammed some clothes into a tote bag and ran back out to the entryway. He was gone. Then she heard a floorboard creak and realized he had walked down the hallway to the girls' room. She tiptoed after him.

"Sam!" She hissed.

"I don't know if I'd sell them." He whispered, nodding toward the darkened room. "They might be worth more to me alive, like their mother." He ran his dirty index finger along her jawline and she held still, knowing if she shuddered he'd punish her.

She grabbed his forearm and tugged him toward the front door, dreading starting over once again. She'd thought she was finished with starting over.

The car roared away, and the town returned to silence.

Elle: March 31, 2008

People often assumed I was a widow. I rarely corrected them.

I welcomed this assumption—some might say I encouraged it. I wore a wide gold band on my wedding ring finger, the kind of band that leaves no question in the observer's mind about what kind of ring it is. I also perfected my phrasing: *I'm a single mother now,* I'd say. Or, *It's just Althea and me now.* Or my favorite, *Life isn't easy without Althea's dad.*

All of these statements were true. It wasn't my fault, or my problem, if people assumed that I'd once had a husband, and he had since died. When anyone asked me directly if I'd ever been married, I answered truthfully.

It was the easiest way I'd found to send a clear signal of unavailability, without wearing an actual sign.

I hated meeting new people—especially men. I blamed this on my small-town upbringing, where we rarely encountered anyone we hadn't known since conception.

What I despised was the initial small talk, the here's-my-life-story, do-you-still-like-me dance. You might think this odd for someone who ran a hotel and met countless guests every week, but that was merely surface-meeting. No dance required.

Whenever well-meaning people asked me where I was from and what brought me to Chicago, I lost all balletic conversational coordination. My answers spilled out in clumsy discord while my potential friend shifted on his feet and stared at the far wall, wishing himself away. I would then pirouette and escape to the safety of the ficus in the corner. The ficus understood.

Feeling like an awkward slow-motion hand-jive performer with a dismal sense of social rhythm, I preferred standing alone in a crowd to standing in a group dodging stilted conversational overtures. Insincerity caused me indigestion.

Strangers sensed my foundering like dogs sensed fear. Somehow, these people already knew I had failed to meet expectations. And so the interrogation would begin.

❊❊❊

Every time I saw a prematurely gray man—think circa-1980 Steve Martin, with less-jolly eyes—I was slammed back into my fifteen-year-old self, defensive and anxious and uber-insecure. My pre-Chicago self. The self I was before I'd left a place where everyone else knew your story better than you did.

But today wasn't going to be one of those days. Today my feet — and mind—would remain firmly in the present. Today was Althea's thirteenth birthday, and I told myself I wouldn't work late again, but I knew I couldn't alter reality. I'd already missed so many milestones in her life, I deserved an entry in the Guinness Book of World Records. What would my title be: World's Workingest Mom?

Her birthday gifts were wrapped and ready, all but one of them stashed under my desk.

I'd planned to leave work early today and surprise Althea, but the semi-annual sales convention week meant longer hours for everyone at the Phoenix Hotel.

I turned the lobby music down a notch, humming along to *Call Me Al* while I waited for the last salesman to finish his phone conversation and let me check him into his room. I'd spent the day covering for Adam, our newest employee, who had called in sick with mono. I liked filling in occasionally, but not at the expense of Althea's birthday.

This I knew for sure: salespeople were too ebullient and way too helpful. If I ran around wasting my energy grinning at everyone and rushing to hold doors for people and helping strangers carry their luggage, all while appearing primped and pressed and ready to hold an audience with the President, I'd collapse. Maybe salespeople were made of sturdier material than the average human.

Although, the superhuman salespeople generally only engaged in surface-meeting. I bet they each had their secrets, carefully guarded behind casual, manufactured answers to polite social questions.

I suppose I, too, was a kind of salesperson, but I was the quiet kind, the kind who respected personal boundaries and relaxed her face once in a while.

The man (Steve Martin's younger brother?) finally pocketed his phone and strode toward the counter, piercing salesman gaze and crisp collar, perfect teeth displayed in a symmetrical smile.

"How's my favorite receptionist today?" His hair was more black than gray, but his facial stubble was all silver.

I couldn't tell if he was trying to grow a beard, or if he was a lazy shaver. Maybe he was going for the magazine-cover look: affected rugged sophistication.

"Happy and busy, as usual," I said. I smiled to soften my tone. "Name?"

His face rearranged itself into a mock frown. "You don't remember my name? I'm crushed." He slumped his shoulders, defining a wiry frame beneath his suit jacket. "It's only been six months since I stayed here last. We had a drink in the hotel bar." He straightened back to his ramrod posture and snapped his fingers, turning the light back on in his hazel eyes.

I noticed they were jollier than I'd first thought.

"You ordered...a whiskey sour, and I told you that was an old person's drink, and you should try a cosmo." He winked.

He actually winked! Could anyone be more arrogant? The cute ones were always arrogant. My stomach fluttered. "I'm sorry, Mr. Jamison—"

"Aha! You *do* remember my name!" He held up one index finger—a personal mini-victory. "I knew I must have made *some* impression on you."

I half-smiled at him, allowing him this scant point. The clock in the lower right corner of the computer screen read 6:00 p.m. Birthday party time. *Where was Mindy?* I wondered. She was scheduled for the six o'clock shift, but she operated within her own time zone. I looked at Joel, then slowly inhaled and exhaled. *Must tamp down impatience.* "Well, you're the last one to check in, so yours is the only name left on my screen. As I was saying, I'm sorry, but I meet so many people here, it's impossible to remem—"

"Oh, but you remember me. We had that drink. We talked. You have a daughter, named...Alyssa? No. Alison?"

I printed out his room reservation sheet and placed it on the counter for him to initial and sign. He stared at the ceiling, palms on the counter. His fingers were long and tapered, the nails trimmed short, no callouses or scars from manual labor. My hands, small though they were, probably looked more workworn than his did.

"Al....Al...Althea!" He snapped his fingers again, pointing at me. "I knew I'd remember it! My ability to recall details is what sets me apart, you know. It's the best skill to have when you're in my business. If you'd like, I could help you develop a system so you can easily recall details about your customers, too. It makes people feel special, when you remember their names." He was in full sales mode. "And by the way, you can call me Joel." He pointed upward, circling his finger to indicate the sound system. "*Call Me Al*. Good song choice."

"Thank you, Joel. I'm—"

"Elle. You're Elle. I remember," he said quietly. He looked at me for two full seconds, then tapped his temple. "Details. They're all in here, cataloged and indexed and ready to retrieve. You're still wearing your decoy wedding ring." He nodded toward my hand.

There was a tiny scar above one eye, a diagonal line through his eyebrow.

"Why mess with something that works?" We looked at each other for a few seconds, and I considered removing my ring right then, but what kind of signal would that send? I might as well wrap my legs around him and ask him to carry me to his room.

I spied Mindy entering the Hotel, a few minutes late for her shift, but early enough to break the spell. "I am leaving--right now." I nodded a greeting at Mindy as she walked across the lobby and through the Employees Only door to stand behind the counter with me. "It's my daughter's birthday and we're having a couple of people over for dinner." Why was I telling him more personal information? I knew he'd just spew it back at me the next time we had a conversation, and he'd probably want a pat on the head for his performance.

"I'm sorry I'm late!" Today, Mindy's hair was black tipped in brilliant pink. "I thought I was relieving Adam." She tugged her sleeves down to her wrists to hide her tattoos.

"He's sick with mono. I'm not sure how long he'll be out." I gestured toward the computer and the stack of files. "I'll finish this last check-in, and then I've gotta run. You should have a pretty quiet night."

Joel glanced at his phone, every gesture a delay. "March thirty-first. Althea's birthday. Got it. Is she turning thirteen?"

Why was it so annoying to me that he tracked these details? And why couldn't he do it on his own time? All my life, at least the portion of it I'd lived on my own, no one had paid me this much intense attention.

I wondered if he cheated on his wife. I didn't see a wedding ring, but that's what cheaters did—removed their rings during sales conventions. How many men had I observed over the years with faint lines or dents where their wedding rings usually rode? Enough to qualify as cliche. Unmarked husbands. Joel Jamison probably never wore a wedding ring, to avoid the whole issue of camouflaging his dented finger.

"Yes, thirteen. You have a remarkable memory." I tapped his reservation form and spoke quickly. "You're in room 339. Do you need more than one key?"

"339. That's auspicious. One key will be fine." He grinned. "Unless you'd like one."

"That won't be necessary, Mr. Jamison."

"Kidding! I'm kidding. And please don't think I talk this way to every hotel receptionist. This is out of character for me. Want me to tell you an easy way to remember my room number?"

I didn't have time to correct him, to point out my Manager name tag and ask him why he assumed I was a receptionist. The clock thundered on, tick and tock. "Sure."

"Threes are always lucky, and anything divisible by three is lucky. My life tends to run on threes. But the easiest way to remember my room number is: three times three is nine. Three-three-nine." His hands shot out, palms up, to illustrate how simple it was.

"Thanks for the tip." I picked up a pile of files and half-turned away, hoping he'd take the hint. "Enjoy your stay."

"One more thing, Elle."

I turned back toward him, just a quarter turn, clutching the files.

"I know you're busy right now, but…are you free tomorrow evening? Maybe we could have dinner. Or something." The word 'beseeching' skated across my brain as I gazed at his face.

I wasn't prepared for this. Most salesmen flirted with me just enough to ensure I'd maintain discretion when I received a call from the person with a matching dent on their wedding ring finger. Of course, most salesmen didn't realize my own ring was a decoy.

"I'll have to check my calendar." What? Why hadn't I said no? I'd expected to hear myself say no, thank you, and have a good evening, but instead my treacherous mouth formed a vague answer with enough hope to keep him hanging. I smiled, but only after my face revealed my private horror.

"Okay, I'll check with you tomorrow. I'm here for four nights, as you know, so…do you like lasagne?"

His tone gentled, and his shoulders relaxed. His ring finger looked like it had never been inhabited.

"Si." I nodded.

"Has anyone ever told you that you look like Jennifer Aniston?"

"Well—"

"I mean, not exactly—but when you are partially turned away, there's something about your eyes and nose that resembles her. And your hair is the same color and style."

"Thank you. I've been told that a few times, but I

can't see it."

"I'm sure it doesn't show up in the mirror—too close and centered. I'll try to capture it on a photo and show you." He grabbed his suitcase handle. "But not today. I've bothered you enough for today. Think about dinner, and let me know." He saluted and sauntered toward the elevator.

I stacked the files on my desk and retrieved Al's gifts and the helium balloon I'd bought earlier, wished Mindy a hasty good night, and ran out the door.

❊❊❊

The balloon floated along, gentle tugs on the ribbon I clutched, while I speed-walked three blocks south, then two blocks west to our apartment building.

I wondered if anyone had yet invented balloon therapy. It's impossible to feel anything but happiness with a balloon bopping along above your head, even when you're running late. It's also impossible to run with a balloon bopping along above your head, because the mental image would make you collapse with hilarity.

My thoughts kept turning to Joel Jamison as I walked. I couldn't seem to reclaim my mind. I breathed deeply even as I scurried along the sidewalks, inhaling the calm quiet of our neighborhood, exhaling the relentless cheer of the salespeople. Every six months, I somehow forgot how exhausting it was during sales convention week. Although, if I wasn't running The Phoenix Hotel and trying to survive sales convention week, I wouldn't have met Joel. Not that I'd ever needed a man in my life. Fickle old things. It would be nice, though, to go out on a date once in a while. I think. I'd never been on a real date, but it looked fun on TV.

By the time I arrived at the door to our building, my thoughts circled so fast I'd worn myself out. I would tell Joel no. He did seem different from other men, and he was the least annoying of the salespeople who attended this semi-annual conference, but I had no vacancy in my life for the complications, commitments and compromises that came along with a relationship.

Our apartment door was unlocked, as it usually was at this time of day. Althea inhabited half of the building, constantly running up and down the stairs to Mrs. Whitcomb's and Malcolm's apartments. We were lucky to have such great neighbors—our own little village within these walls. I could hear Malcolm and Mrs. Whitcomb talking and laughing.

I flung the door wide and pushed the balloon into the room. "Happy birthday!"

Everyone turned toward me and started talking at once, greeting me and taking the gifts from my arms.

"Oh, my land, girl! You look like a walking birthday party!" said Mrs. Whitcomb.

"Mom. A balloon? Really? I'm thirteen." Althea smiled to soften her faux-snarky comments.

"Yes, you're aging by the second. Enjoy the balloon before the wrinkles start forming," I told her.

"I'm almost as old as you are!" Althea took the balloon and tied it to the wine bottle on the table.

"Fifteen years is fifteen years," said Malcolm. He squeezed my arm. "Salutations, Ms. Marchand."

"Good evening, Malcolm. The table looks great! Thank you for setting it. I'm so sorry I'm late."

"We all pitched in a little, dear. None of us has anyplace to go, so don't fret." Mrs. Whitcomb smiled. "Now have a seat here. I poured you a glass of wine." She pulled out my chair.

"Thank you. Wine sounds fabulous." I kicked off my shoes and removed my jacket before sinking into the chair. "I feel like it's *my* birthday—what a nice way to end the work day."

Malcolm and Mrs. Whitcomb settled into their chairs, one on each side of Althea.

"Did you have a long day, Mom?"

"Not bad—the sales convention people checked in today. Adam has mono. Typical Monday. Next week is the women's yoga retreat, so a vast improvement is on the horizon."

I sipped my wine and looked at Althea. She'd braided a section of hair and applied a pale pink lip gloss. She looked like an innocent twenty-year-old.

"How was your day, Al-Critter?"

"I had a great day! No one at school remembered

that it's my birthday, Mrs. Whitcomb made me a great snack, Malcolm didn't have any new books to catalog. It's like I had a day off." She grinned. "I think being thirteen agrees with me."

"The secret to a happy life," said Malcolm, holding up his crooked index finger, "is to make sure every age agrees with you."

"That is so true! Oh, my land, I can tell you, seventy-eight agrees with me just fine. Although, I do sometimes wish I could be sixty-five again. That was a great year." Mrs. Whitcomb smiled and sipped her wine. The rhinestones on her glasses sparkled.

"Well, that was thirteen years ago!" Althea reached over and squeezed Mrs. Whitcomb's arm. "Of course it was a great year!"

We all chuckled.

"Now that we're all present, let's commence serving." Malcolm stood and scooped the stew out of the crock pot. He placed a slice of the French bread he'd brought alongside each bowl of stew. "Where are Roberta and young Courtney this evening?" he asked.

"They couldn't make it. Roberta's sister is having a family dinner." I'd met Roberta at work, when we cleaned rooms together for one summer season, and we'd been close ever since. Now she was a yoga teacher and counsellor, helping single mothers (many of them teens) find jobs and support themselves. Courtney was a year younger than Althea, and the girls had a strong friendship as well.

After dinner, I cleared the plates and placed a stack of gifts in front of the birthday girl. She tore into the first package, from Mrs. Whitcomb. A pair of knitting needles and yarn.

"The plain white yarn is for practicing, and the nice yarn is for your first real project." Mrs. Whitcomb said. "We can start lessons whenever you're ready."

"Thank you! I've been wanting to learn how to knit," said Althea. "I want to make a sweater."

Mrs. Whitcomb laughed. "You might want to start with a scarf, dearie. Or a hot pad."

Malcolm gave Althea a book, as always. "It's *Little Women*!" Althea said as she ripped open the paper. "My teacher talked about this book the other day, and she told us that Louisa May Alcott is one of her favorite authors. Maybe I'll write a book report on this, and get extra credit!" She looked at Malcolm, and I could see she loved him like a grandfather. "Thank you, Malcolm."

"My pleasure, my girl." He nodded and grinned, revealing his piano key teeth.

Al always saved my gifts for last. She tore through the paper and held up a black dress with cap sleeves, then grabbed a pair of black pumps from the box and dangled them so we could all see them. "Thank you, Mom! I love it all."

"Keep digging," I told her. She found the play tickets in the bottom of the box. "We're going to have a girls' day," I said. "We'll go to the museum of your choice, dinner downtown, and the play."

"*Chicago*!" she shouted. "I have tickets to *Chicago*. We're going to see *Chicago* in Chicago. That is so cool." She sounded breathless. "Thank you, Mom."

"Oh, my land, that play is a bit...gritty," said Mrs. Whitcomb.

"It is." I nodded. "But I think Al is old enough now. Like she said, she's almost as old as I am!"

Althea laughed and straightened her back.

"I've already read the play, anyway, and my friends have seen it," she said.

"Children grow up fast these days," said Mrs. Whitcomb.

"I have one more gift for you," I said. I ran into my bedroom to retrieve the professionally wrapped package from the closet, then ran back to the dining room and held it out. "I splurged."

She unwrapped this one slowly. "Ooh, is this what I think it is? Is it what I've been asking for?" Her hands moved as she talked, fingers slipping under the tape, prying the carefully folded layers apart. "The box is a little bigger than I thought...Wow, Mom. A laptop? Are you sure we can afford this?" She was still, looking at me with an adult seriousness.

I hoped she wasn't disappointed to see a laptop instead of an iPhone.

"Yes, I've been saving for it. We have a pretty good

nest egg, Al-Cheeks, so don't worry. However," I held up one finger, "I'm not yet ready to pay for Wi-Fi. You'll have to come to the hotel when you want to use the Internet."

"That's great! That will be great. I'll go to the hotel more often. Ooh! I'll be like those business people who are always staying there. So cool! Thank you so much!" She launched herself out of her chair to hug me.

"I know you wanted an iPhone," I told her. "But the monthly fees are too high. It's just not practical. I hope that's okay."

"It's fine." She tempered her disappointment with a smile. "I can still text Courtney from my laptop, when I'm on Wi-Fi." She lifted the computer over her head. "I have a MacBook! Yahoo! I'm going to bring it everywhere."

"How did you escape the technological revolution?" Malcolm asked me. "It seems everyone is perpetually focused on their electronic devices, and you don't even own one."

"Not a priority." I sipped my wine. "I wasn't even introduced to a computer until I worked at The Phoenix. I have a laptop, but only because I'm going to school and they required it."

"Mom's the only parent in my class who isn't on Facebook," said Althea. "And she's the youngest mom there is! Everyone else's mom is old and wrinkly."

Everyone laughed at this.

I glanced around the table at our ersatz family and thought, not for the first time, that family is made up of those you've chosen, rather than those you've acquired in a biological crap shoot.

The phone sounded like it always did, shrilling an alert with no ominous overtones.

"Hello?"

"Is this Ellen Marchand?" The voice was unfamiliar, pinched and proper.

I hadn't been called Ellen in years. The sound of my full name made me feel ten years old.

"Yes it is."

"Hello, Ellen. I'm calling about Jack Marchand. I understand you're his next-of-kin."

I sat down and listened. I wondered if I cared.

Althea: April 1, 2008

On the last day of my normal life, I figured it out. All the stuff you don't know? You don't know that you don't know it. Cuz you don't know it yet. And what you don't know that you don't know, well, that can be bad.

Especially when the stuff you thought you knew turned out to be not quite true. More like a second cousin of truth.

Believe me, I can be the empress of drama, but that's my right. I'm thirteen, and I know my rights.

It's a short list.

The day began a sheep, and it was a great disguise. I didn't even see the wolf coming until he pounced. It was Tuesday: I walked to school at my regular pace, throwing in a skip every few steps so I could keep up with my feet.

I usually walked with my BFF Courtney, and when I say usually, I mean the three or four days per month when she perfected her appearance early enough to be on time. So today I walked alone. Courtney is 63%

brainiac, 19% funky fashionista, and 18% whimsical. She's 100% my friend, though. We're dedicated like that.

The birdsong sounded jazzy with the traffic back beat, the sun felt warm on my face, and squirrels gossiped while they performed acrobatics, defying death each time they crossed the street. Except the ones who didn't make it to the other side.

On Homeless Hal's corner, he grinned and good-morninged me like always, and when the light turned red he popped the daily trivia question.

"Do you know why Chicago is called the Second City?" His yellow eyes looked clearer than usual. He wiped his nose on his ragged sleeve.

"Because it's second to New York?"

"Nope! That's what most people think. It's because after the Chicago fire, the city was rebuilt. So now it's the *second city* to grace this fine landscape." He extended his arm in a wide arc, encompassing the entire urban area.

Hal's signature scent wafted toward me. A cloud of unwashed human, stale alcohol, and despair. I coughed to cover up the gag I couldn't prevent.

I paid Hal with a smile and rushed across the street, gratefully inhaling car exhaust.

I've always known I'm different from the other kids—I'm old for my age, and close to my mom. Most of the other kids don't live with their dads either, but at least they know who their dads are. One girl does live with her dad—her mom actually moved away. I can't imagine that, but I *can* imagine having a dad. Someone who would call and ask about my day, ask questions, share stories. Someone who would teach me how to drive, how to build shelves, how to play sports. Someone who would care and listen and stay.

I power walked home from school and waved at Hal as I passed his corner. He'd relocated to the other side of the street by then, to take advantage of the sun, and he grinned back at me, splitting his beard open to expose the few teeth he still had. He'd lost his hat again. Sometimes someone would pluck it off his head, leaving him shivering and diminished. I imagined the hat-stealer short and punky, dressed in black and always running from himself. Whenever I noticed Hal's bare head, I crocheted him a new hat, for which I received a growly "thanks, peanut" when I dropped it in his lap.

Hal's corner is only three blocks from our apartment, and they're the prettiest three blocks on my six-block route. Oaks and chestnut trees extend their leafy arms to form an almost-tunnel over the street.

Our building has six apartments—two on each floor—and we live on the second floor. Malcolm lives below us, and Mrs. Whitcomb lives above us. The other tenants are less like family and more like across-the-landing neighbors—people we greet at the mailboxes, people we say "excuse me" to when we meet on the stairs, but we don't really know them. Two of my favorite people on earth, Malcolm and Mrs. Whitcomb, have lived in our building longer than my mom has. The other tenants tend to treat our building as a starter apartment, leaving after a few months or a year. Sometimes one of them has a young child or a baby, but usually they're young couples, full of energy and plans, and they barely notice us long-timers.

I liked our building. Its perfect position on the north side of the street provided maximum sunlight through the large windows on the street side, great during the dark months of winter, and the balcony was on the back of the building, where we sat outside in the shade in the summer time. It was a brick building with clean lines—I heard a real estate agent say that during a property tour—and I loved living here.

I ran into the lobby and checked the mail, certain this would be the year I'd get a birthday card from my dad. Every year I had two birthday wishes: 1. That no one would remember my birthday and 2. That my dad would magically realize it's my birthday and send me a card. The card hadn't come on my birthday, but there was still time. The mail could take longer than he thought, it could arrive here today, the day after my birthday.

For the thirteenth year in a row, there was no birthday card. Nothing magical had happened during the year and I still had no dad. I hadn't really expected it. I had only expected it a tiny little bit.

I paused at Malcolm's door to knock four quick knocks, a slight pause, then two more quick knocks. This was Morse code for "hi", and it let Malcolm know I was home from school. Upstairs, I flipped open my phone and texted "Home from school" to Mom. I glanced into Mom's closet for a hot second, but I didn't touch anything. Mrs. Whitcomb would panic and worry if I was late for my after-school snack and daily chores.

Today was Tuesday, which meant it was time to wipe down the kitchen and the bathroom. I'd been helping Mrs. Whitcomb with her housecleaning chores since I was in Kindergarten, and it was one of my favorite times of day, ranking right below helping Malcolm catalog his library.

"Hello, Althea!" Mrs. Whitcomb always greeted me as if she'd been waiting all her life to see me again. I felt like a celebrity every day. I often wondered what Mrs. Whitcomb would do if I didn't visit her.

"Hi, Mrs. Whitcomb. How are you doing today?" I smiled my sunniest smile, competing with the real thing outside the window.

"I've had a good day, child. A quiet day. If I'm not mistaken, it's your first full day as a twenty-four-year-old! How's life treating you?" Her lips and nails were always done in a matching shade of pink. Today's shade was tulip bright.

I sighed, slumping my shoulders to show her how disappointed I was about not yet being twenty-four. "Mrs. Whitcomb, you know I'm only thirteen." I grinned at her. "But you know what? I'm only one day in, but I know it's going to be the best year yet." I straightened my back to appear taller.

"Oh! I'm sure you're right." She clasped her hands together in preparation for a standing ovation. "Would you like to eat before or after doing your chores today?"

"I'll whip through the chores first." I grabbed the cleaner and the roll of paper towels, and ran into the kitchen. I wiped down all of the kitchen cupboards, the counter and the table, then ran into the bathroom and cleaned the toilet and countertop and sink. Cleaning speed records must have smithereened that day.

"Today's snack is avocado salad," said Mrs. Whitcomb, serving it with a flourish. She had more energy than you'd expect for an antique person, but she did take a short nap most days, just before I came home and did her chores for her. She had short white hair and glasses with rhinestones on them, and she always wore pantyhose under her pants, which she called slacks. She had sandals in every color, but only one pair of boots: black.

I ate her delicious salad, which was really just chopped up avocados with feta cheese sprinkled on them, drizzled with vinaigrette. One sliced grape tomato perched on top. Mrs. Whitcomb could have served food in one of those fancy restaurants where there's more plate than food, every dish photograph-worthy.

***

I couldn't go home without visiting Malcolm first. I hoped he wouldn't detain me. My legs felt like ropes, or maybe cables, and I'm sure I could have run ten miles to reach Mom's closet, but instead, I bounced down two staircases to Malcolm's library. He actually lived in an apartment with the same floor plan ours had, but he had so many bookcases it looked like a library. And every book was filed with Dewey Decimal precision, tiny typed stickers on the spines. Just like a library. Malcolm's apartment was my favorite because it wasn't plain like ours, and it wasn't full of knickknacks like Mrs. Whitcomb's. It showcased books. Glorious books!

If I was ever in a coma, and I woke up and didn't know my own name, if I was lying in Malcolm's apartment I'd know exactly where I was by inhaling the scent of old and new books. The heady ink-paper-glue smell that should be featured as a cologne—who wouldn't buy that?—calmed me and energized me at the same time. Mom said this is what it felt like to be centered, which she was after her yoga class with Roberta, and when the yoga retreat people stayed at her hotel. She said she was half off the bubble the rest of the time—but I couldn't tell.

"Salutations, Fledgling." Malcolm's greeting rarely changed.

"Good evening to you, fine sir." I curtseyed because Malcolm's old-fashioned like an English butler, and he liked that sort of thing. At first you might have thought he's a prude, but he's just a highly functioning intellectual. Mom said he's esoteric. He didn't wear a vest like the butler you might have pictured, but he always wore a button-down shirt ironed to a crisp.

"How was your stint in academia today?"

"It was…tolerable." I looked up at him, from the top of my eyes, and grinned. "I used my vocabulary word. And, I have a grammatical faux pas from Mrs. Warczinski for you." If there were such a job as a grammar referee, Malcolm would wear out his whistle.

He clapped his hands together once, the hint of a

smile turning up one corner of his mouth. "Let's start with the vocabulary word." He glanced toward the ceiling. "Exercise my recollection. Was today's word 'flumadiddle'?"

I laughed. "The word you assigned was 'amanuensis'."

"Aah, so it was." His eyes glinted in the library light when he looked at me.

I felt a giggle climbing up through my belly, but the library was no place for giggles.

"Mrs. Warczinski assigned us to write an essay about what we're going to do this summer, and then we had to read it aloud. So, I wrote about my position as your amanuensis, and I explained that even though it's a year-round job for me, I'll have longer hours in the summer."

"Mag*nifi*cent!" He held his arms up, bent at the elbows, and I could almost hear the crowd roar-whisper 'she scores!'.

I stood still, smiling at him, waiting to see who would break first.

He did.

He tapped his ear. "I stand before you, prepared for your elucidation." His voice sounded like a judge or a priest, booming and distinguished.

"I feel I should warn you, it's a small one. It's teeny tiny. Probably not worthy of writing down." His look told me he'd reserve judgment until he'd heard the entire story.

"First, I had to explain what 'amanuensis' was, and then she asked me why I didn't just call myself a 'secretary'. I told her the word secretary is pedestrian, and if someone is a secretary the least they could request is a better title."

Malcolm harrumphed, most likely remembering the time he'd given me a similar explanation.

"And then I said, 'besides, I love big words—the bigger the better—so why not use them?' and she said, 'Well, I can *contest* to your love for big words!' and I was the only one who laughed. So I tried to turn it into a cough." I demonstrated my laugh-cough for him.

It was library quiet for three beats.

"A tri*umph*ant observation." He beamed, his face the color of parchment, his teeth long and shiny in the lamplight. "And I think it's worth noting. Please transcribe this scenario into the Grammatical Faux Pas Index."

I retrieved the ledger from the shelf and opened to the latest page. I neatly penned the date and began printing out the scene to provide context for the faux pas. This was the 103rd entry.

Malcolm and I loved lists, and we kept lists of everything. His lists included various indices, an inventory of his books, and a list of dates he wanted to remember each year. My lists included interesting words, things I wanted to buy, and ideas. Some ideas were my own, and some were ideas I'd borrowed from others (mainly Malcolm). My favorite list was my List of Tolerations, which was my way of handling things I didn't like.

My chest felt tight and my legs wanted to carry me away as I wrote. I had to get back to the closet, even though I already knew what was there.

***

Two days ago, the day before my birthday, which would have been my birthday if it wasn't for leap year rudely pushing my birthday out an extra day, I snooped. I told myself it would be my last crime, but that changed when I found what I found.

I felt bad rummaging around in Mom's closet, but I couldn't wait any longer. I had to know if I was getting a smart phone for my birthday. Every other kid in my class had smart phones, most of them iPhones, and if I wanted to call anyone I had to go off someplace so no one could see my lame-o flip phone. It was better to pretend I didn't even have a phone, and borrow someone else's to avoid flipping out my phone like the actors on 90s sitcom reruns.

People were oddly protective and stingy with their phones—most of them would only lend me their phone after they punched in the digits themselves, as if I'd break the screen if I touched it. Then they'd stand there with one hand out, ready to receive the phone back, and they'd check messages or whatever as soon as it was back in their hands. I doubt they missed anything during my thirty second convo, but apparently smart phones needed to be checked and rechecked twice a minute or so.

Even Courtney has an iPhone. I'm the lamest thirteen-year-old on the planet.

If Mom didn't buy me an iPhone, I would buy one myself with the money I'd made working for Malcolm.

Mom's closet was not as organized as mine. Her clothes weren't filed by color, or even by season. Every time I opened her closet door, which wasn't very often, I wanted to rearrange her entire wardrobe. Don't get me wrong, Mom was organized in her own way, but I must have inherited my organizational skills from my unknown dad.

Sometimes I felt like my dad was a ghost or some kind of specter, part-person, part-spirit. Cuz it just seemed wrong that he didn't know anything about me, and I didn't know anything about him, but we have this solid biological connection.

I reached under the clothes and swept my arm back and forth, but my fingers only met shoes. Piles of shoes. I knew the sandals were mixed with the clogs, the boots mixed with the flip flops. I tried not to think about it.

I parted the clothes, and that's when I noticed the manila envelope standing up at the back wall of the closet. It was pinned by a white strappy sandal and a heavy clog. I carefully slid it up the wall and pulled it out without disturbing the shoes.

The envelope contained a ticket stub, a scrap of fabric and some other papers and cards. The stub was dirty and wrinkled, and looked ancient. It said:

Jam Productions Presents
GRATEFUL DEAD With Special Guest
Soldier Field, Chicago, Illinois.

Sat., July 8, 1995, 6:00 p.m.

Under that, it had a list of rules: No cans, no glass, no alcohol, no flash cameras, no video equipment of any kind. No camping, no overnight parking, no vending.

Wow. I held in my hand the actual ticket stub from the actual Grateful Dead concert my mom had attended on the one and only wild weekend of her entire life. It was soft, probably from almost fourteen years of handling. I smelled it. It smelled grubby. It smelled like old sweat and dirt and rotted leaves. It smelled like history. That concert was the reason Mom moved to Chicago, the reason she named me Althea, the reason she's never really dated anyone for the last thirteen years. If Mom's life was a book and I had to write a report on it, that concert would be the turning point of the story.

Maybe I wouldn't always be the kid with no father. My heart galloped and a whooshing sound filled my ears. All these years, I'd watched and waited for a birthday card, and a pile of clues had been here the whole time. Should I ask Mom about him again? Would she tell me more this time? Maybe I should try to find him on my own.

I heard the front door open and shut.

"Al-chicky? Are you home?" Mom called out. "I'm sorry I'm late!"

My hearing suddenly returned and I gasped, just like they do in the movies. I shoved everything back into the envelope. I stuck the envelope back in the closet, but it wouldn't slide all the way down to the floor because the shoes were in the way. I hoped if Mom looked, she'd think the envelope had been nudged by her shoes.

I scuttled out her door and into mine, then answered. "I'm in here, Mom. Homework." I tried to sound tired of the whole homework routine without sounding like I was complaining about it.

I'd have to wait until my birthday, a full twenty-four hours, to discover whether or not Mom thought I was worthy of a smart phone. I'd also have to decide what to do about the pile of clues wedged in the corner of her closet.

Elle: April 1, 2008

I tried to forget Jack Marchand's sudden re-entry into my life. I tried to pretend I hadn't received the call from the hospital, that maybe I'd imagined it or dreamed it. It had taken me years to feel sturdy without his support, like I was a broken reed in the wind, and I'd finally figured out how to splint myself back together and stand tall again.

One phone call brought back the anxiety, the unease of not knowing if, when or how he would speak to me. The certain uncertainty of having a family, yet belonging to none. The phone call hadn't even been dialed by Jack himself—that would have been too personal for his taste. According to the books I'd read on the subject, Jack displayed classic passive-aggressive behavior: he loved to tell Stella what to say to me, and he was so cruel in his third-party way, I'd asked Stella years ago to stop passing on his messages. It took me days to recover from his referring to Althea as "the little bastard" or "Ellen's biggest mistake".

After hearing those comments, in the early years of Althea's life, I would throw myself into work. I developed a signature cocktail—the Phoenix Rising, a concoction of whiskey, powdered sugar and vanilla, decorated with a small tissue-paper bird on a swizzle stick. I started giving each guest a goody bag as a gift when they checked in—the salespeople received a sales-oriented book or magazine and a couple of local restaurant coupons; the yoga retreat ladies received some tea and coupons to a local yoga class; the writers' guild received high quality notebooks and pens. I changed the contents of each type of goody bag every six months or so, enjoying the challenge of finding new items that fit within our budget. I added a reading nook to the lobby, complete with a bookcase filled with books guests could borrow with no return date. I taught the maids to leave a personalized note in every room after they cleaned it, unless the room wasn't booked for the next night. The maids also learned how to fold towels into animal and flower shapes.

I wrote to him back then, like Ruth advised, each month—carefully worded epistles designed to convey my success and Althea's extraordinarily advanced abilities. When I received the first few letters back in the mail marked Return To Sender, unopened, I stopped putting a return address on the envelope. Sometimes I included photos of Althea—never of me—and sometimes I sent a newspaper article about The Phoenix or some neighborhood event, hoping to demonstrate how full and rich our lives were, away from the brutal economic depression of the UP, away from the town busybodies, away from him. I suppose it was my own passive-aggressive way of retaliating.

When I stopped putting my return address on the envelopes, they stopped boomeranging back to me, but after a couple of years—by then it had been six years since I'd driven the failing S-10 south on Highway 41—I tired of not knowing if he opened my letters and read my words. I wanted to stop writing, but by then it was a compulsion. I was the out-of-control child jumping up and down, crying, "Look at me! Look at me!" and as far as I knew, he wasn't looking.

I switched to post cards. I printed large, neat letters on the back, so he would read my message without intending to, before he realized who had written it. One day, as I let go of the post card and watched it slip into the post box on the corner, I saw myself as a caricature of grief and disappointment. I pictured my post card making its way to the former cabin that housed the post office in Iron Falls, gossipy old Mrs. Cunningham reading my pathetic pleas for attention before tucking it into Jack's box with a smirk on her face.

How many townspeople knew I was writing him

postcards? The thought of my post cards being the subject of morning coffee klatsch conversation turned my stomach, and I finally stopped writing to him.

I followed the advice I read in *Your Parents Aren't Your Fault* and forgave Jack. The healing was nearly instant: I felt lighter, stood taller and smiled more, I gained energy, I was more patient with Althea and I stopped obsessively double-checking the mail for a response from Jack.

Life was pleasant.

Now I saw the truth: It didn't matter how many affirmations I wrote each day. It didn't matter how many self help books I studied. It didn't even matter how fiercely I strived for a reliable level of self-confidence, or that I'd finally started taking college classes.

All of this disappeared like so much vapor when I heard his name.

The cloak of my reverie had insulated me from sound —the phone rang two or three times before I flinched back to the present moment.

"Hello?" I was out of breath as if I'd jogged up two flights of stairs to silence the shrill ring.

"Hey, Ellen. Just wondering when to expect you." It was Stella, steady as ever, acting as if this new reality featuring Jack communicating with me, albeit through a stranger, was standard operating procedure. I pictured Stella as I always did, a stoic twelve-year-old with a smattering of freckles and a blunt pixie cut.

"How is…Fossil?" I nearly choked on the last word, unable to call him Dad, settling for the smidgeon of respect his nickname afforded.

"Not good. He's still asking for you, and I need to know what to tell him." Stella sounded like the frontline receptionist she was, charged with gathering information from reluctant subcontractors or material suppliers.

"I haven't exactly decided if I'm coming home or not." My words started out slow and built speed, so the last four words came out in a rush. I was breathless again.

Stella gasped. "What? Not *coming*? What is this about, Ellen?"

"Al has school. And so do I—my semester is nearly over."

"Weak excuse, Ellen. Besides, you could teach the class yourself. People don't go to school to learn how to run a business after they've already been running one for years." Stella sounded frustrated. "Look. Dad *asked* for you. For *you*. He is willing to reconcile."

"I don't know if I want to reconcile." My voice sounded flat. Deflated.

"You've been so busy all these years being Miss Independent, proving you didn't need Dad or anyone else, you never thought about what you'd do if Dad ever needed you." Silence. "He needs you now. He's not a bad person, Ellen. He's still the same Fossil."

"Wait, which is it?"

"Funny. I think he regrets letting you leave, but he can't say that. You know how he is."

My silence stretched to an uncomfortable length.

Stella was relentless. "You *have* to come. Look, Ellen. If you don't come home for Fossil, come for yourself."

"What do you mean?" The minute I asked that question, I knew I'd lost.

"If you don't see him now, when he called—invited—*beckoned* you, you will regret it. This opportunity has a short shelf life, Ellen. You'll wonder forever whether you should have faced him, and you'll never be able to find out." She spoke fast, cramming all of her words in my ear before I could stop her.

Stella still knew I craved closure like a bee craved pollen.

I sighed. "Damn it, Stella, where did you learn to be so persuasive? I don't want to come. I dread seeing Fossil, in any setting, let alone in a hospital room. And he didn't even call me himself—he had a nurse do it."

"You're acting like him."

"What?"

"At the very least, don't dismiss him like he dismissed you. Life is already heavy. Don't add this to your burden."

The silence stretched out on the phone line. It crawled all the way from Iron Falls to Chicago and back again.

"I'll see what I can do. Thanks for calling. I guess."

"You're welcome. It's the right thing to do, coming home."

"How come you never left, Stella? Why are you still there?" I asked softly.

"You know I'm not a leaver, Ellen. I'm a stayer. I stay and stay and stay. Mom left Fossil, then you left him—I felt like I had to stick by his side. Someone had to."

My jaw clenched, making it difficult to spit out the words. "I didn't *leave* him. He evicted me."

"He wouldn't have made you leave. You know that. He was angry and disappointed, probably in shock. He felt like he had lost control of his life. You know how he lashes out, yells at people, then he has to live with what he said." We were breaking our rules. Stella never defended Fossil, except through her silent, obstinate refusal to leave his side, his business, his town. Our tacit agreement to avoid this subject was the fragile thing that allowed us to communicate and remain somewhat true to our younger sisterly selves.

"Well, he lived with it, alright. So did I. And Althea."

We were silent for a moment, each of us letting go of this conversation before it consumed our relationship. I had left, she had stayed. These were the facts, and we couldn't change them. Not today.

"Let me know when you're on your way. Safe travels." She set the receiver down quietly and I sat for a moment, the phone to my ear, listening to nothing. I felt like I'd swallowed a brick.

I needed to call Roberta and see if she was still willing to loan me her car, but first I'd make another call.

I popped two Motrin and dialed the phone. Joel answered on the first ring.

"Well, hello, there." His voice was deep and smooth like a soft blanket, enveloping me and warming me up.

"How did you know it was me?"

"How do you know I knew it was you? That's how I always answer the phone." He chuckled. "Are you calling to tell me you want to go to dinner tomorrow?"

"My, you're presumptuous." Where did this flirty voice come from? I didn't know I could sound like that. Maybe it was the anxiety about Fossil talking. "No, I'm calling to tell you I have to go home tomorrow. My dad's sick." This last sentence sounded so well-adjusted and functional, I wondered if someone else had said it.

"Home home? Like up north?"

"Yep." I paused. "I'm sorry, Joel. If I can have a rain check—"

"Of course you can. Don't even worry about it. We'll make plans next time I'm in town. I hope your dad feels better soon."

It jarred me to hear someone who's never met Fossil call him my dad, as if I were a normal girl with a healthy father-daughter relationship. Roberta's dad visits her often, sometimes unannounced. He stops by for coffee, diagnoses her car troubles, builds bookcases and cheers for her victories, minimizes her defeats. One night I shared my history with Roberta over a bottle of Captain Morgan Silver, a rare indulgence for both of us. Tears plopped into my drink as I exposed my ugliest scars. We talked until the sun came up the next morning, then crashed on her couch and slept until the moon rose over the neighborhood, full and bright and wearing a knowing expression. Courtney and Althea, mistaking our hangovers for a bad case of the flu, made us tea and toast and put cool cloths on our foreheads.

Roberta said, at the end of my sad tale, that it was Fossil's loss. She said Fossil might have been strong, but he wasn't brave. She said I must have inherited only the best of Fossil and Elyse, and that I was the most loyal, faithful, stubbornly staunch person she'd ever met.

Roberta always knew what to say.

February 28, 2001

Dear Althea,

I feel silly writing you a letter. You're just learning how to read, and you might never read this. You can't read it until you're older, anyway, because this letter will tell the truth. Not some glossed-over, wishy washy, half-made-up truth, but the real truth. Because a girl should know about her mother's life, even the difficult parts. It's the difficult parts that make the difference. And I'm almost 21 years old, so even though I've been on my own since I was 15, I'll be a real adult soon and I want to tell you how I got this far.

Ruth said I should write the story of my life so far so you can read it some day, and she's so wise and practical. She saved our lives. But I should start at the beginning, which was before I knew I needed saving.

Once upon a time, way back in 1979, there was a man named Jack Marchand. He lived all by himself in a big house in a tiny town many miles north of Chicago, across the State line in Michigan's Upper Peninsula, in a place called Iron Falls. Everyone who lived in the UP was called a Yooper, and Jack was the Yooper poster boy. He owned a construction company and hunted all year round, fished when they were biting, and drank beer every evening.

He always said he was perfectly content in those days by himself, building his business and living alone. He was starting to grow old, already halfway through his forties, and his black hair was turning white, but he had sharp blue eyes and could still carry a 180-pound deer carcass on his shoulders without breaking a sweat. Everyone called him Fossil because he was so strong and cemented in his ways. Until...

One cool August evening, when Fossil was eating his dinner at the bar and minding his own business (Fossil always used that phrase when telling this part of the story), a tall, skinny woman with long blonde hair walked in and asked him if he wanted to shoot pool. Her name was Elyse Elizabeth Nussbaum and she was less than half his age. The connection was instant, like touching two wires together and creating a bright, sizzling spark. They shot pool all night until the bar closed, and Elyse won more than she lost, even though Fossil said he gave her his best game—she was that good.

Elyse was beautiful, like a princess in a fairy tale, and Iron Falls had no hope of adjusting to her presence. She was full of energy and carried that spark with her everywhere, flashing it with her eyes when she smiled, trying hard to fit in with townspeople who'd been there for five generations.

There's something you should know about the UP, Althea:

It's a cold, hard place to live, and sometimes it seems as if everything is against you there—the weather, the high prices, the low wages—and people tend to stick together to survive. But when people have known each other since before birth, when their great grandmothers played together long before there were Barbie dolls to play with, those people don't want to let just any old interloper from out of town—especially one so beautiful and graceful and friendly—walk in and be part of the circle. That's not how things work in the UP, even if you're married to Fossil. I'll get back to this later.

The townspeople, when they looked at Elyse, saw a hologram, a phantasmagoria. A flight risk.

Pretty soon Elyse found out she was pregnant, and in June, 1980, I was born. Yes, I started out in this world with two of the best parents a person could imagine. I inherited substantial longevity and strength from Fossil's side, and exotic beauty and charisma from Elyse's side.

My "good" half, the couple-hundred-year-old roots Fossil had wrapped around the town, afforded me easy acceptance from the townspeople despite the half of my questionable lineage from who knows where. Elyse may or may not have come from California or Minnesota or Connecticut, or maybe she'd lived someplace else altogether before walking into the bar and meeting Fossil. Elyse was a woman whose story changed to fit the situation. She was from nowhere and everywhere, easily mimicking our local accent and erasing her own.

In Yooper terms, I was a half-breed.

Back to the story. Life went on, Elyse grew a round belly again, and during a fierce blizzard in February 1982, Stella was born. She was almost born in Fossil's truck. The roads hadn't been plowed and it was snowing so hard Fossil couldn't see. Elyse kept grabbing his hand when she had a contraction, and he said it was a miracle they didn't end up in the ditch when she did that. He parked on the sidewalk at the hospital, blocking the front door with his truck, and he ran around and lifted Elyse out—first waiting until her latest contraction ended —and carried her in, like Prince Charming. "There's no time for a wheelchair!" He shouted at the nurse. "Just show me where her room is! We've got no time, no time!"

Fossil's phrase, 'we've got no time, no time!' became a family mantra we used whenever we were running late.

My hand is cramped up like a claw, Al-bug. I'll continue this tomorrow—

Althea: April 2, 2008

My name was an incomplete sentence: Althea Imogene Marchand. Adding punctuation, it changed to Althea Imogene, March and. March and what? March and fall, march and die, march and twirl? March and April?

I wished I could drop the 'and' from my last name and become Ms. March, like the girls in Little Women. I would have had legitimate namesakes, albeit literary rather than live, and my name would have formed a complete command. But the way it stood, Marchand, it was as if someone got bored and didn't bother to finish their thought.

Jerry Garcia named me. People reacted to this news in one of two ways. If they were over 30, they'd ask, "*the* Jerry Garcia?" And if they were under 30, they'd ask, "Jerry *who*?"

The story of my name was one of my faves, especially when Mom and I were comfy on the couch late at night and it was dark and quiet and I asked her to tell it to me again. And again.

My mom, during the one wild weekend of her entire

life, went to a Grateful Dead concert. The last one held in the world. There, she met my dad and they heard Jerry sing *Althea* and, when she discovered she was pregnant shortly thereafter, all she could think was, "Jerry was singing that song to me, telling me to name my baby Althea". She heard that song before I had ears. She said she still thought the world revolved around her then. She took what she regarded as Jerry Garcia's advice and named me Althea. Every time she calls my name, she remembers that crazy trip to see the last Grateful Dead concert.

She said she's been gratefully alive ever since.

It's a great story. The only trouble was, there were giant holes in the story and my dad fell through one of them and she wouldn't pull him back in. She always said she didn't remember his name or where he was from, and all she knew was, he never called her and she never saw him again.

I'd been up since 4:30, silently turning pages in my mom's old photo album. When she left her home in the UP, she took her clothes, the money she'd saved babysitting, and this photo album. The first page showed her mom, pretty and young, standing next to her dad, hair almost as white as his teeth, but you can see he still had lots of energy. Mom said he was prematurely gray.

The next few pages contained photos of babies, first one and then another, held by the pretty woman on the first page. When the second baby appeared, the first one was nearly two years old and tried to hog the camera. She photo-bombed nearly every picture of her new sister, her hair tangled and her face sticky-looking. Mom's mother was Elyse, but she's no longer with us. That's what we say, anyway.

There were many, many photos of the two girls: playing together, laughing together, crying, sleeping, eating. They always wore mismatched clothes. I liked to study the backgrounds to try to get a sense of their lives. What would life have been like with yellow flowers on the kitchen wall? How could anyone who had handmade pine paneling in the living room be unhappy? I would feel nothing but cozy and loved if those walls were my background. Judging by the looks on the girls' faces, that's what they did feel, before they knew any better.

After my mom was about five years old, the page layouts abruptly switched from amateur pictures lovingly placed on each page to hastily tucked school photos, showing Mom and Stella when they began Kindergarten. Stella started Kindergarten when she was three years old because Mom dragged her along on the first day of school, and she told the school Stella couldn't stay home alone.

"Stella was so smart, she kept up with me every year," Mom said when she told the story I never got tired of hearing.

Mom and Stella were a team before Mom and I were a team, and they were a force to behold. But Mom said the difference was, she'd never leave our team like she left Stella. I know she felt more guilt than a gold-plated crown about leaving Stella, but she said she did what she had to do for her new team, because I was on the way and I wasn't about to wait for anyone.

"She graduated high school at fifteen. Fifteen was a big year for both of us." This was when I had to duck out of the way so Mom wouldn't ruffle my hair. I didn't have much of a hairstyle—shoulder-length, slightly stringy dishwater blonde hair—but I hated it being out of place.

The photo album was concrete proof that people could withstand changes larger than anyone could imagine. It proved my mom's strength and her ability to go with the flow. I hated that expression: go with the flow. Why couldn't life flow around us? Why did everything have to change?

Jack Marchand was in the hospital. Invading our lives from afar, from his sick bed. I didn't know how to react to this news. I didn't know if I was supposed to care. I didn't know if it was even the tiniest bit normal that all I felt was a kind of numb bubble in my stomach when I thought about him.

Not only that, I was a little bit mad at Jack Marchand. How would I find my own dad when Mom's dad was hogging all of the space in my life?

***

I let the school day flow around me—I did not go with the flow. I didn't even greet Homeless Hal on my way by, but he didn't notice me anyway because he was busy spouting trivia and collecting money from strangers as I slinked past his corner.

After school, since it was Tuesday, I was supposed to

dust Mrs. Whitcomb's knickknacks, but she had a doctor appointment so Dust-day was officially canceled for the week. This was okay with me, even though it was a change to our routine, because I wasn't sure I could withstand Mrs. Whitcomb's cheer today.

I let myself into Malcolm's apartment, immediately comforted by the bookcase sentinels. Surely nothing could go awry within these literary barricades.

"Salutations, Fledgeling," said Malcolm, his voice a dignified boom from the other side of the bookcase on my right.

"Good afternoon, Malcolm." I tried to sound happier than I felt.

"Any news on your mother's father?"

I peeked around the bookcase to smile at him. He looked up from his book, waiting for my answer.

"No, and I haven't heard from Mom all day. She has the sales conventioneers there this week, so she's probably jumping and running all day."

"Aah, the conventioneers." When Malcolm said it, he made them sound silly, like mousketeers or something. "I received three new books today, and they're ready for you to process." He gestured toward the desk where the books were stacked, and resumed reading.

Grateful for the distraction he offered, I grabbed the books and sat down at Malcolm's desk. He had a computer so I could look up the proper Dewey Decimal Classification, and an old-fashioned typewriter so I could type each book's code numbers on a label and affix it to the spine, library-style.

Three and a half minutes into my research, my restless legs propelled me out of the chair and over to Malcolm's side. I bounced lightly on my toes, suddenly unable to expend enough energy.

"Malcolm, why is the Dewey Decimal System only used for books?"

Malcolm held up a finger while he finished reading, then inserted an index card and clamped the book shut. "What do you mean, Fledgeling?"

"Well, wouldn't it be nice if the Dewey Decimal System also categorized other things, like movies, events...maybe even people! Then we would know at a glance who we're supposed to hang out with. If there was an evil demon hiding inside a pleasant cover, others would know it by glancing at his code. Then he wouldn't be next to a romantic novel, and their pages wouldn't get...you know...woven together."

Malcolm looked as if he was considering the advantages of my ridiculous idea. "I like the premise," he finally said, "but I think the negative implications outweigh the positive ones. Think for a moment what might *not* have transpired, had those pages not woven together."

I looked at Malcolm, my face growing hot. We'd never come this close to talking about sex before, and that whole topic was distracting me from his words. I turned slightly so I could see outside through the sliver of window across the room and thought about what he said.

"Oh." I gasped, just a little, because this was no place for drama. A little goes a long way in a library. "I get it. There would be no...baby books."

"You are cor*rect*! There would be no progeny. Present company notwithstanding, your premise might tidily solve one of our planet's most urgent problems—overpopulation—but I suppose that is a moot point."

It was time to change the subject. Silence ballooned between the bookcases as I thought.

"Where did you go to college, Malcolm?"

"Child, I went to the only University in existence! Harvard." He paused. "How old are you now?"

"I'm thirteen."

"Aah yes, thirteen and two days. It's about time you started planning your Harvard matriculation and subsequent edification."

I smiled at him, hoping he knew what I couldn't say without feeling somehow disloyal to a man I'd never met: I wished Malcolm was my grandfather. This feeling was definitely not a numb bubble, and I wouldn't mind if he hogged all of the space in my life.

"I'll worry about Harvard after I deal with Jack Marchand."

"You are wise, Fledgeling. Everything will come together in its own time."

***

The envelope was pinned to the wall of my brain, itchy and nagging. The minute I got home from Malcolm's, I carefully liberated the envelope from Mom's dark closet once again. My new MacBook had a camera, and I took a picture of each item in the envelope:

Ticket stub—front and back
Piece of fabric
Torn piece of paper
Three photos
Two receipts

I saved all of the photos in one file, marked Clues, then I reassembled everything and carefully wedged the envelope back against the closet wall behind a brown clog and a pair of slippers.

Back in my own room, I opened each photo and studied it on the screen. The torn piece of fabric looked like it was from a black T-shirt. One side was straight, like it was the bottom hem, and the other sides were torn and ragged, almost as if a dog had taken a bite out of it. Not much information contained in the shirt.

The photos were of Mom and Stella. One pic had Mom, Stella and another girl; one had Mom, Stella and two boys, one standing really close to Mom; the last one had Mom, the other girl and the two boys. All of the photos had the same background, some kind of dirty yard with colorful bits all over it. The sun was shining, and lots of people were walking by or sitting or lying on the ground behind them.

One receipt was from a restaurant I've never heard of —Papa's Pizza—and the other was from a Walgreen's store. Someone had purchased a pair of sunglasses.

The torn piece of paper had some light pencil markings on it. I increased the contrast and sharpened the image until I could make out the words: Roy Harrison (Farm Town) 608-935-22. The rest of the number was ripped off the page. It looked like a kid wrote it—not a little kid, but not an adult, either. The zero had a jaunty slash through it and the eight was written like two precise circles balanced on top of each other. My head snapped up as I realized what I was studying on the screen.

Roy Harrison was my dad. And I was going to find him.

Althea: April 3, 2008

"So, are you going to see your grandpa or not?" Courtney asked.

"My grandpa?" I dropped my head and studied the cracks in the sidewalk. How could I have a grandpa when I didn't have a dad?

"I heard my mom tell your mom that she should go or she'll regret it."

We walked to my house after school. Courtney's mom and my mom were good friends, maybe besties, and if we had to drive to the UP, we'd borrow Roberta's car for the trip. She's the only one Mom would be comfortable asking, and she probably wouldn't even have to ask, because Roberta would insist on loaning it to her even though Mom hadn't driven anything as long as I could remember.

Roberta had a kind of sixth sense from all her years as a yoga instructor.

"Oh, you mean Jack Marchand. It's funny to think of

him as my grandpa."

"Yeah, well, it's weird that you call your grandpa Jack Marchand. Who does that?" Courtney adjusted her glasses with a nudge of one finger, then moved them to the top of her head.

"You would, if you never met your grandpa before. Mom said we don't have to call him dad or grandpa because he didn't earn those titles, and we don't call him by his nickname either because that shows affection and respect and we're not sure if we have either of those feelings for him." I parroted Mom's monologue without thinking. It made me feel kind of bad, talking about Jack Marchand when I didn't even know him. I hated it when people talked about me behind my back.

"It must be some kind of crazy, not knowing your own grandpa." The hot pink lacy shoelaces threaded into the eyelets of her faux-combat boots caught my eye with every step, little flags waving hello from Courtney's shins.

"It is. But I don't know my own dad either, so I guess it's normal in my family. We don't do dads."

Courtney touched my forearm. "At least you have good friends. I don't think you're crazy." She smiled. "Not too crazy, anyway."

We walked on, stepping over debris and tree roots and listening to the traffic. One of my favorite features of Chicago was the constant noise. It was never completely silent. My life had a built-in soundtrack.

"What's his nickname again?" Courtney asked.

"Fossil." Did my dad have a cool nickname, too? Would I ever find out?

"Weird! Grandpa Fossil. So, are you going?"

"I don't know. Mom hasn't mentioned it since the night of my birthday, when we got the call."

"The UP is full of savages." Courtney had her serious face on. She grabbed my arm to make sure I was listening. "There are no laws and people just do what they want. Hardly anyone lives there, because it's so cold all the time and there aren't any jobs and there's more trees than anything else. Deer and skunks are everywhere. And wolves and bears." She shuddered.

"My mom never said there aren't laws or jobs."

Courtney dropped my arm and shrugged. "She probably didn't notice cuz she grew up there. Just like we don't notice stuff around here."

I nudged Courtney's shoulder. "What don't you notice?" I grinned at her. She dreamed of being a forensic scientist. She watched the news and followed crimes. She was obsessed with NCIS and she practiced for her future job by studying people at a glance, then reciting their distinguishing characteristics. If I was ever in a position where I'd need to identify someone in a line-up, I hoped I'd somehow borrow Courtney's ability to notice details.

She grinned back and put one finger in the air. "Score one, Al. Anyway, in the UP, they survive on sticks and berries and try to outrun the bears. If they don't freeze to death."

"It can't be that bad, but if we go, I'll let you know what it's like." I wondered if my dad had ever been to the UP.

"You should take pictures of the people. I wonder if they look like us."

We skipped in tandem across the sewer drain, then stopped, paused, and jumped over the curb onto the sidewalk. We'd started this routine when we were in first and second grade, and it still made us laugh when we performed it at random moments.

"Of course they do! My mom is from the UP, silly. She looks perfectly normal."

"Hmm. I heard they all have beards and wear flannel shirts all the time." Courtney twisted her mouth in disapproval.

"Maybe not the women."

"Maybe." She looked doubtful.

Courtney Louise Jade. Could there *be* a more perfect name? She's blonde, too—a perfect Barbie shade, with natural caramel colored undertones, and of course her eyes are green like her last name. They should have been hidden behind her glasses, but she sticks them on top of her head most of the time so she doesn't feel like a dork. She's a year younger than I am, but we hang out because our moms are so close and we live only seven blocks apart. Her mom never got married, just like my mom didn't, and our moms frequently discuss the wisdom of avoiding divorce by steering clear of its main cause: marriage. Courtney saw her dad once or twice per month. He planned activities so they wouldn't have to sit and stare at each other—they went to museums, shows, Navy Pier, and once they even drove to Standing Rock State Park and hiked the trails.

I didn't know I was going to say anything to Courtney, until I said it, and then I realized I knew all along that I couldn't hold it in.

"Want to know a secret?"

Courtney nodded and leaned toward me.

"I found out who my dad is," I whispered.

Courtney stopped walking and grabbed my elbow.

"What? How? Where?" Her eyes wide, she looked around behind her. I knew she couldn't see all the way across the street, because her glasses were still perched on top of her head. "When?"

"I'll tell you about it after Mrs. Whitcomb's." I held one finger up to my lips as we approached the apartment building.

"Oh, come on." She stomped one foot. "How am I supposed to wait that long?"

It was Thursday, which meant laundry day. If I was ever blindfolded and shoved into Mrs. Whitcomb's closet, I'd know exactly where I was by the scent of black licorice and roses. Her place smells way better than most old ladies' houses. Not that I've been in any others. I can just tell.

Courtney kept bugging her eyes out at me and wagging her head one way or the other while we folded Mrs. Whitcomb's laundry. She even beckoned me into the next room, but I ignored her. She made me nervous and I didn't want Mrs. Whitcomb to suspect anything.

Mrs. Whitcomb served brie and crackers while we folded the clothes, leaving us no private time whatsoever.

It was two full hours after school when I was able to

retrieve the laptop from my closet. We sat on my bed and I opened my MacBook and clicked on the file. Courtney sucked her breath in and glanced at me.

"Wow," she whispered. She stared at the screen. "Who's Roy Harrison?"

"He's my dad." My voice sounded watery and I almost looked behind me to see if someone else had said those words.

"Are you sure? You have evidence?" She'd entered detective mode.

"He *has* to be. Look, you know how every now and then my mom mentions her one wild and crazy weekend?"

"The Grateful Dead concert?" She turned from the screen to look at me so we could roll our eyes together.

"Yep. And she always says Jerry Garcia named me, and I was born 9 months after that concert—look at the ticket stub." I talked faster and faster, unable to wait for the words to fully form before pushing them out of my mouth. "I found all of this stuff in an envelope in my mom's closet, and I took pictures of everything and put it all back."

The room was so silent, it hurt my ears. I don't think either of us was breathing. Courtney pulled her glasses down onto her nose and studied the screen.

"And why would she keep all this stuff? Why would she keep some scribbled piece of scrap paper with some random name on it?" I stared hard at Courtney. The blood vessel at my temple throbbed and my face got warmer and warmer. "Because the name isn't random." I spoke this last sentence slowly and deliberately, like a lawyer in a courtroom.

"Because he's your dad," she whispered. "Wow. Oh wow." She bent toward the computer and clicked through the photos, looking at each one again and again. "He's got to be one of the boys in these photos."

"That's what I thought, too. I know Mom went with her friends Ariel and Boyd, and they're brother and sister. I can't tell which boy looks like Ariel, though."

She studied the photos side by side, zoomed right into their faces. "No, I can't tell. Same hair color on all three of them, and same eye color, I think. It's hard to say for sure. Even their jawlines are different. We need a police sketch artist or something."

"Well, we don't have a sketch artist. But this could be your first case. You could be the lead investigator."

She straightened her back. "I accept the assignment. Was anything written on the backs of the photos?"

"No. I flipped them over, like, a million times."

"Have you looked on the internet yet?"

"A little. I'm sharing Malcolm's wifi. There are, like, a million Roy Harrisons. And that's just in the US, and how do we even know he's still in this country? He could be from Canada. He could have moved to Europe."

"Yeah. But I bet he's still around. I don't know. What's the Farm Town thing all about? Is he from a town with that name?"

"Google doesn't know."

"Okay. I'll start checking. I wish we had access to the databases they have on NCIS."

Courtney scrolled through the photos again and studied the torn phone number note one more time. “When we find him, can I meet him?”

I liked it that she said when, and not if, like she had faith in our cyber sleuthing abilities, of which I had none and she had a tiny bit more than zero. But I didn’t like that I hadn’t even thought that far ahead yet, and I had no real answer for her question.

November 10, 1993

Sam whistled along with Canned heat. I'm goin', I'm goin', where the water tastes like wine.

"Please." She spoke softly. "I really need the restroom."

"Hmm?" He cut his eyes over at her. "Can't you make it to the dealer's?" His fingers tap, tap, tapped in time to the song.

She blew on her hands. The heater hadn't worked in months. November rain today. The worst kind of rain, in her opinion. Chilling and shivery.

"There's a gas station right up here." She pointed off to the right. "I'll be quick."

"You are some kind of high maintenance." He pronounced it main-tain-ants. "I can't put gas in this thing now. Haven't you ever traded in a car before? You always leave it with a quarter tank or less."

"I'll just run in." Her lower lip protruded, and when he looked at her, she bit it hard with her teeth. "If you don't stop, you're going to have a biohazard in here, and they're not going to take this old jalopy."

Sam hit the steering wheel with the heel of his hand. "For Chrissakes." He spun the wheel to the right—wax on—and they careened into the station, then he whipped it to the left—wax off—and braked hard at the curb. "Well?"

She cleared her throat. "Could I have a dollar? I don't want to just use the restroom—"

He dug a five dollar bill out of his pocket and threw it at her. "Bring back the change. Every penny."

She opened the door and climbed out. A Mercedes Benz pulled up at the pump, and the driver slumped out the door. His suit jacket had been discarded and his tie was askew. She wondered if he'd be interested in swapping troubles. Rich people must have simpler problems.

"And hurry up." Sam shouted. "We're supposed to be at the car dealer's ten minutes ago."

She waved and hurried into the station, her heart beating so hard the clerk could probably hear it over the noise of the radio. She wiped sweat from her upper lip and ran into the empty restroom, shakily locking the door behind her. She didn't bother wiping the dirt from the mirror—she knew she wouldn't recognize the dull hair and sallow skin skating across the glass.

She climbed onto the toilet, careful not to lose her footing and land in the water, and cranked open the window. It didn't open far enough for her to fit through, but she was prepared for this. The flimsy hinges were easily broken out with her pliers, which she'd been carrying in her purse since her last attempt had been foiled by the same style of window. She pried out the hinges, pulled the detached window inside, and set it in the sink.

The opening, when she was standing on her porcelain step stool, was almost armpit-height. She lifted one foot and eased her weight onto the windowsill, then maneuvered her other foot through the opening and slowly worked her lower body past her hips, then past her chest, then eased her head out sideways and lowered herself to the ground. Her hands were sweating. She forced herself to think calmly, to focus on breathing, to move carefully. She peeked around the corner of the building at the GrandAm and saw Sam get out of the car and head toward the gas station.

She heard him yell at the clerk. "There a woman come in here a minute ago?"

Mr. Pinstripe was climbing back into his

Mercedes. He looked defeated—deflated—and she knew this was her only chance. She sprinted across the concrete to his passenger door and yanked on the handle, expecting it to be locked. Expecting Sam to run out the door and tackle her. Expecting lights or sirens or bullhorns or all three.

She opened the door and dove onto the passenger seat floor.

"Who are you?" Mr. Pinstripe sounded startled and put his hand on the horn. He was younger than she'd expected, but still old enough to be her father.

"Don't! Please!" She shout-whispered. "Please. All I need is a ride away from here. I escaped from the man in that GrandAm over there." She pointed.

"Should we call the police? What has he done?" The car smelled like sweaty pistachios and leather. He watched the rear view mirror for a few seconds, but must not have seen any movement inside the station. She studied the back of his hand as it rested on the gear shift.

"I'll tell you everything, but please, no police." She held up two fingers. "Scout's honor. I'll give you everything I have. Well, it's only five dollars." She wouldn't look away from his face. "But you can have it all. I just need a ride to—anywhere. I can't run from here! There's no place to hide. He'll run me down." Her hands shook

"Okay, okay. I'll take you down the road, and we'll sort this out. You'll tell me the whole story, and you'll want to pursue legal action, I'm sure."

He drove her directly to his office where he took her statement and set the prosecution of one Samuel Clark in motion.

Six months later, after Sam was convicted and sent to prison, she married Mr. Pinstripe and she never looked back.

Most of the time.

Althea: April 4, 2008

I studied the photos intently. I wondered if I was clinically obsessed—if that was even a real term. It seemed unhealthy to be so focused on one thing, but then again, everyone said my generation lacked focus. So maybe my freaky focus was actually a regular level of focus, like people used to have before everyone stared at their iPhones all day long and checked email seventy-eleven times per day.

The phone rang—the real one on the wall, not the lame-o flipper in my pocket. It startled me so much I jumped to my feet in one motion.

It was Malcolm.

"Fledgling," he said, pausing until I answered, "would you please avail me in the library at the next opportunity? I have a project for you."

"I'll be right down." My voice echoed loudly in the empty room. I studied the antique map of Chicago's Near North Side neighborhood pinned on the wall and wondered how many people never knew their grandpas. When that map was created, I bet most people knew their grandpas. Back then, divorce wasn't cool, and women couldn't make it on their own. What happened to women who were never married, but had a baby? Hmm. They probably had to keep living with their parents, or find someone to marry. But at least the kids would have had grandpas and grandmas.

I wondered if I'd get to meet Grandpa Fossil. I hoped so, but at the same time I hoped not. Like Mom always said, we made it this far without any grandmas and grandpas—why would we need them now? Mom also said the only person you can count on is yourself, so make yourself strong. She said it's important to stand by your word, even though most other people don't. I think she learned most of this stuff in the self-help books she read. She read them obsessively—hopefully with a regular amount of focus.

It was so tiring, being half of a family of two. Big families must have had it easier because they could split the weight of the past between more people.

I skipped down the stairs to Malcolm's library and called out as I entered. The scent of book pages and lemon Pledge, as always, provided a comfort I'd never been able to name.

"Aah, Fledgeling. You're expeditious today." He smiled —the smile that shows his approval and pride in me— and I caught a dim glimpse of Malcolm as a grandpa. How grand would that be—to have Malcolm as a grandpa? He'd probably insist on being called

Grandfather—a more dignified term than the pedestrian Grandpa.

Malcolm showed me the new books he'd acquired, and I set to work typing the Dewey Decimal labels and accompanying catalog cards. We worked together to shelve the books and before I knew it, two hours had passed.

"Have you finished reading *Little Women*?" He asked, turning from the bookshelf where he'd neatly lined up the spines. I handed him the dust cloth and he swiped it across the books.

"Yes! I forgot to tell you—it was a cool story. My favorite part was the way they talked." He raised his eyebrows and waited for me to provide examples. "Like, when they said 'I had a capital time' and 'make yourself splendid'."

"Ah, yes. The Victorian phraseology. *Little Women* is where I first read the phrase 'fortuitous concatenation of circumstances'." He spoke this with one finger up, in a deliberate, snooty voice.

I laughed. "That's a good one! I'll try to remember it. They said 'dreadful' all the time, too. I think the word 'dreadful' should be brought back into regular conversation."

"So it should, Fledgling. We shall commence using the word 'dreadful' in conversation today." He looked like a band conductor as he swung his arm for emphasis.

Refined, I thought. That is one word that describes Malcolm.

"Did you know Louisa May Alcott supported herself

and her family with her writing?" He asked.

"No." I searched his face, waiting for him to tell me why this was interesting.

"In the Victorian era, it was virtually impossible for women to make a living. Ms. Alcott lived for just over half a century, but she accomplished much. She socialized with Ralph Waldo Emerson and Henry David Thoreau." He pronounced those names like they were celebrities, or people I should know.

"Did everyone use all three names back then?"

"I suppose the upper crust used all three names. Sometimes one's social status wasn't defined by money —sometimes it was defined by intellectual abilities. Many upper crust socialites were destitute creatives."

I thought about that for a minute. "Sounds more fair than worshiping people just because they have money. Some of them have money because they're lucky—not because they earned it."

"Exactly!" Malcolm lowered himself into his ancient oak chair, probably the first office chair to have wheels. "A society based on money alone, especially when that money is awarded to dullards and troglodytes for their plebeian activities, will self-destruct."

He was rolling now, presenting his views lecture-style. I felt lucky to be his audience of one.

"A society requires industrious attention, ingenious inventions and intellectual curiosity. And—money. It requires," he paused to wink at me, "a fortuitous concatenation of circumstances. And we, as citizens, must create and facilitate those auspicious circumstances."

***

When Mom came home, she didn't even take off her coat before telling me, "Stella called. It sounds like we need to go up there." I couldn't tell if she was happy or sad about this fact.

"Okay—when are we leaving?"

"We'll leave the day after tomorrow. I am *not* rushing home for Jack Marchand. I'll write a note for your teachers—bring your homework with you. Bring a couple of books to read, too. And your laptop. There won't be much to do." She looked like she'd been running for as long as she could remember, and now she had to stop and accept stillness, but all she wanted to do was keep moving.

"Are we taking Roberta's Corolla?"

Mom nodded. "I'll get it tomorrow, and we'll leave early Saturday morning." She looked hassled, frazzled and not the least bit dazzled. "It's a long drive, Al-kins. A long drive. To nowhere."

"We can play road games!" I tried to cheer her up with fake excitement.

"Sure we can."

Her smile was so thin, I walked over and hugged her. The last thing Mom wanted to do was visit her dad, and yet, we were going to drive hundreds of miles to see him.

Would I even *want* a dad, once I found him?

March 2, 2001

Dearest Al,

I'm writing to you at the dining room table. The sun is shining today, and I'm so warm I could curl up and sleep.

I don't remember life without a sister. Those early years, in my mind, are filled with light and giggles and fun projects. Elyse had an artistic streak, and she would set up painting stations for us. I remember wondering when Stella learned how to hold a paint brush, then wondering when I'd learned the same thing. Water color was our medium, and we would paint the special paper Elyse set up for us, then we'd paint our fingernails and toenails so they would look like hers.

Elyse wanted us to call her Mum, in the English tradition. She said it sounded less crass than Mama or Mommy. I didn't know what crass meant, but I remembered the word and looked it up years later. See, Elyse said she tried to fit into the local community, but she always made little remarks like that, little darts aimed at the UP culture or even the American culture. I never considered this before, but maybe Elyse was from Canada. Or England.

Now that I think about it, many things about Elyse were contradictory. Or maybe my memories are poorly preserved. I remember eating jam and bread, jam and scones, honey on toast. You probably think I'm making that part up—but I really did eat that many carbs! We each had a special cup for tea, which was served weak and lukewarm. Sometimes it was warm water and lemon.

So we were two princesses, with a Mum and a Dad. Our world was small but happy, busy but sequestered. Elyse had no real friends in town and seemed intent on making our little circle its own society. We three girls did the shopping and cleaning every day, sometimes stopping to see Fossil at work, then we'd help Mum prepare dinner. She had us stirring and measuring at early ages, always patient with our clumsy toddler movements. I remember baking cookies, kneading bread, stirring soup on the stove from my perch on the kitchen stool. We even had aprons. We must have looked like two miniature homemakers. Mum called us Stellie and Ellie.

Then one day, January 5, 1985, she was gone. I woke up that morning and she wasn't in the house. Stella still slept in a crib even though she was almost three years old, and when she woke up she had to go to the bathroom so I dumped all of her clothes in one big pile next to the crib and helped her climb out. She landed on the clothes, safe and sound. We kept busy all morning making toast and pouring juice, washing our hands and brushing our hair. We played dress-up for a while.

We were fixing butter and sugar sandwiches for lunch when Dad's truck screeched to a stop outside and he ran in the house, eyes wild and hair even wilder, sticking up like he just rolled out of bed. I remember wondering where his ball cap was, and thinking something really bad must have happened for him to lose track of his hat like that.

He gathered us into his arms and held us, even after we started wiggling and begging to be set free, and he cried. I didn't know dads could cry, but there he was, tears running down his face, and he didn't even try to hide them. He kept saying he was sorry and we would be okay, and he would take care of us.

The next few days remain blurry in my memory. There were lots of people—the townspeople, entering our lives when we needed them most—bearing casseroles and frozen lasagnes and loaves of homemade bread. Pots of soup. Teddy bears. We must have received sixteen teddy bears that week from well-meaning people we'd never met, who had known Fossil all of his life. I remember wondering how everyone knew where we lived, because no one had ever visited us before.

"I met your daddy in the hospital when we were born," one lady told me, her smile so wide she nearly swallowed her own face. Her hair was a funny shade of blonde, like Cheerios, and it was big and puffy and shellacked. "He and I are one day apart, and our cribs were put next to each other in the nursery. We even had a double baby shower because our mothers were best friends." She folded her hands on her knee, proud of these facts, but I couldn't figure out why they were important. "Now,

you two," she went on, "are just a teeny bit older than my grand babies! Isn't that something?"

I guess it was something, but I had no idea what.

At some point that week, Stella stopped talking, except to me.

I was four and a half and Stella nearly three when we lost our Mum. I learned to say "she's no longer with us" whenever anyone asked, which wasn't very often because in a town like Iron Falls, everyone knows everything practically before it happens, so people don't ask questions like that, even to make conversation. They mainly talk about the weather.

Fossil hired an assistant to help raise us, and he threw himself into his work. Heather came over every morning, bursting with energy and fun ideas. Her main goal was to get Stella to talk, but I remained Stella's interpreter until we went to school. Stella started school with me that fall, trailing after me into the Kindergarten room on the first day. At first I think the teacher was just placating us, allowing Stella to sit with me, but when Stella started doing her own work, faithfully copying the alphabet and matching colors and shapes, the teacher started treating Stella like a real student.

That's another thing about small towns in the UP—things like regulations and laws are handled on a case-by-case basis.

Stella started talking again just before deer season, but she still clung to me like a marshmallow on a stick.

After we started school, Fossil would leave work early on Fridays and pick us up, and take us to dinner at the bar. It's not a bar like we have here in Chicago—it's more of a family-style bar with a dining area. Lots of people went to dinner on Friday nights, and this must have been Fossil's way of socializing us. The waitress always knew what we were going to order, and the other diners greeted us or came over and asked us how we were doing. Everyone knew Fossil, and everyone knew what had happened.

Life went on like this, with Heather acting as a big sister/junior mother for years. Fossil put her on his construction company payroll with the title Administrative Assistant, and he paid her well to clean our house, cook our meals and maintain our daily schedules. She drove us to school and picked us up every day except Fridays, and she left our house after serving dinner. Sometimes she stayed and ate with us, sometimes she even spent the night on the couch. Heather was the one we called when we needed a ride, or lunch money, or if we'd forgotten our homework.

The weekends were spent with Fossil, road hunting, hanging out at the construction office or driving to Houghton to pick up building supplies or tools.

My best friend was Ariel Heinonnen, and the three of us became inseparable. We spent the night at each other's houses and read Stephen King books out loud to each other, taking turns chapter by chapter, so we could all experience the book at the same time without being scared to death. We walked all over town together and people called us the Three Musketeers.

Ariel's brother Boyd was three years older than we were, and sometimes he would come over, too. Fossil hired Boyd to keep an eye on us when Heather needed a day off, figuring *three girls might get into less mischief if a boy was in charge. Boyd was the original geek—the other kids over pronounced the d at the end of his name, so it sounded like Boy-**Duh**—and he wore the requisite nerd costume, complete with dorky glasses and plaid shirt. Back then, being a nerd was the farthest you could possibly be from cool, and Boyd was all nerd.*

He taught me how to play chess, and we'd sit for hours pondering our moves, discussing strategies, while Ariel and Stella did each other's makeup and curled each other's hair.

It was during one of these chess games that Boyd said, "I heard about your mom—is she coming to visit you?"

I was instantly freezing cold, my entire body rigid like the re-rod Fossil used to reinforce concrete. My stomach flipped over. I couldn't breathe. "That's sick, Boyd. Mom died, like, almost nine years ago. Don't even tell me you didn't know that." My voice sounded as flat as I felt. My stomach contents hovered, half-regurgitated, at the back of my throat.

"No, that's what I thought, that she died all those years ago, but my mom was telling my dad that Elyse called Fossil, and asked about the girls."

"What?" My body was numb by this time, and I couldn't see or hear anything but Boyd. I didn't know Ariel and Stella were standing behind me.

"Mom said everyone knows Elyse left. She waited until after Christmas that year, and she left Fossil a note. She moved back to wherever it is she came from." Boyd's voice was gentle, but his words cut like razors.

"No, this can't be right." I shook my head. I couldn't figure out how what he was saying could be true. "It can't be true. She died, Boyd. People brought food and teddy bears. People—people smiled at us with pity in their eyes, and patted our heads, and—they gave us breaks, Boyd. Like when Stella started school and they just let her stay. Or when we wore the same clothes for two weeks one time, and everyone said 'it's the Marchand girls' like it was perfectly normal. Or when Stella didn't talk—did you know she didn't talk? For months? Except to me. She only talked to me, in a whisper like she had laryngitis, and everyone said 'that's okay, sometimes these things happen'." My voice rose until I was shouting. "When? When do these things happen? When people die, *Boyd." I was starting to hyperventilate, and when I turned around, Stella was standing there, stunned, the color of clam chowder, tears tracking down her face and dripping from her chin to the floor.*

I was thirteen and a half when I found out my mother wasn't dead. Stella was nearly twelve. We were in eighth grade.

I need another break, Al. I'm feeling a bit shaky.

Elle: April 5, 2008

Roberta's car came with an ashtray full of change and dollar bills, and an extra pair of sunglasses tucked above the driver's side visor. There were no other extraneous items floating around her car—she kept her car like she kept her house and her person, organized and austere. Minimalistic.

I appreciated the impersonal feel of the debris-free interior—it was bad enough I didn't own a car, but at least I could tell myself this was more like a rental than a loan from a friend. There was no map in the glove box, so I had to rely on memory to navigate, and I knew I didn't need the map itself so much as the comfort seeing a neatly routed plan would provide. *Besides,* I told myself, *her map, if she had one, would probably contain only Illinois. I need Wisconsin and Michigan.*

Thankful my grip on the steering wheel hid the

shaking in my hands, I started out. The sun shone with a renewed strength, promising summer, growth, redemption. Everything went smoothly for the first half-block, until I nearly put us through the windshield when I braked for the stop sign. Althea cried out and I stammered an apology.

"I'll get better," I told her. "It's just been a while since I've been behind the wheel. It'll come back to me." I hoped my words comforted her. I didn't believe them, myself.

"That's okay, Mom." She clutched the dashboard with one hand, and the door handle with the other. "Take your time."

I grinned. "You want this eight-hour trip to take twelve? Is that it?"

"I'm prepared for an all-nighter." She smiled, but didn't unbrace herself.

Within the first mile, my braking improved and we didn't have to rely on our seat belts to prevent concussive injuries at every stop light.

"Things are looking up—I don't think we're going to get whiplash."

Althea smirked and nodded, and gradually loosened her grip on the dashboard and door handle and sat back in her seat. "I was looking forward to being immobilized so I could catch up on my reading."

"You've always been my silver lining girl." I smiled at her. "It probably sounds odd to you, but I drove more miles before I was old enough for a license than I've driven since I moved to Chicago."

"Well, you could teach me how to drive on the way, and then I could log some pre-licensed miles of my own."

I looked at her from the corner of my eye. "I don't think so, Al Andretti. Times have changed."

"Kidding, Mom. Chill." She was looking at me the same way, from the sharpest corner of her eye.

It seemed to take hours to leave the city. Did I really drive on these roads thirteen years ago? Evidently, a scared, surly, stubborn fifteen-year-old girl had more confidence than a cynical, wise, realistic twenty-eight-year-old woman. I snickered inwardly, wondering when I'd started considering myself wise. My memories of that long-ago drive didn't include worrying about the traffic, or the blasé pedestrians, kids on wobbly bikes or errant dogs springing out in front of me. I didn't recall worrying about where I would sleep, what I would eat or how far the truck would take me, or even how I'd know when I arrived at my destination.

I was driving away, back then. My mind was focused on the past, on putting wide space between myself and my dad, on the problem I was so sure I was solving. Today, I'm driving toward—what? My old problems? No, I'm driving toward the prevention of regret, and I'm going to drive it into the ground, as Stella implied.

The last time I shopped in the boutiques lining the

streets of Near North, I bought a tiny canvas print for my desk at work. It proclaims my new mantra: *Don't look back; you're not going that way.*

I am *not* making a U-turn.

Finally, north of Milwaukee, the line of cities fell behind us and I settled in for some highway driving. We needed gas soon, so I watched for the first gas station on my side of the road. I set Roberta's cruise control and relaxed slightly, allowing my back to touch the seat for the first time since we'd embarked on this tour of duty. Try as I might, I couldn't shut off the sarcastic comments bouncing around my head.

I hadn't been north of Chicago since 1995 when I'd rolled into town broke, broken, and dirty enough, I'm sure, to appear homeless. Which I was, I suppose. I'd never considered myself homeless before, but technically, I was just that for a week or so.

My sudden speed adjustment to a near-crawl caused Althea to look up from her book.

"What the heck?" She said.

"I just didn't want to rear-end this farmer." I gestured toward the behemoth farm equipment ahead of us, piloted by a tiny man perched high on the rig. The machine, whatever it was, took up more than half of our lane.

"What's he doing on the road? Is that legal? He's going to kill someone!"

"Oh, this is normal. We're in the country now. You

won't see this in the western UP so much, but Wisconsin has many farms. He's probably moving this thing from one field to another."

"It looks like it could stab a person. Or a whole crowd, all at once."

"Mass impalement." I shuddered.

"Where are all the buildings? I've never seen this much…land…with nothing on it."

"There are barns, silos, houses. There's even a person walking down the road!" I pointed these things out as I spoke. "The land is pretty, isn't it? The rolling hills and the straight rows of crops. It's very soothing."

"I think it's freaky. I don't know if I could ever get used to seeing so far. It's weird. There should be buildings, and people, and cars. This is way different than seeing farm scenes on TV."

"Well, instead of buildings and people, we've got barns, cows and odd businesses." I read the sign aloud as we passed it: "Eggs and Sheet Metal."

"What does that even *mean*?"

"I guess, if you're in the market for some sheet metal and you're also out of eggs, you only need to make one stop. The owners must not want to put all of their eggs in one basket."

"You're cracking yourself up, Mom." Althea couldn't help but crack a smile herself, I noticed.

"Pun intended?"

She rolled her eyes and grinned.

Before long, I grew tired. Tired of staring out the window, tired of concentrating on the road, tired of anticipating the greeting awaiting us in Iron Falls. My eyelids felt like they were made of lead. My neck held all the strength of cooked spaghetti and my head bobbed sharply.

"Wine and house painting," Althea said.

"Hmm?"

"That sign back there. Another diversified business. We also passed one that said 'Cheese and Wood Carvings'. Are you okay?" She was looking at me, concern in her eyes.

"I'm getting tired. I can't believe how tiring it is to drive, even on a road like this with barely any traffic."

"We're almost to Green Bay," said Althea. "Didn't you say that's about halfway? Let's stop at a restaurant so you can take a break. We'll still get there today."

I navigated the hair-raising cloverleaf off-ramp and pulled into Olive Garden, the first restaurant on my right, and we took a well-deserved respite from the road.

The rest of the trip was almost too short—we crossed the bridge from Marinette to Menominee and entered Michigan, and suddenly we were driving along the familiar tree-lined highway that featured Iron Falls as one of its wide spots.

The urge to put the car in reverse was nearly overwhelming. I could drive back to Chicago backwards, I thought, using only my mirrors and stopping only for gas.

"Wow, it's true what Courtney said."

"What did she say?"

"There are more trees than people in the UP." Althea sounded awed by this revelation.

"Oh, the trees outnumber the people here several times. Hundreds of times."

"Do all the men have beards? And wear flannel shirts?"

My attempt to curtail my laughter resulted in a cough-snort. "Not all of them. Bearded flannel-wearing males are a common sight, though."

"Are they savages?" She whispered.

"For Pete's sake, Althea, where do you get these ideas?"I looked at her, and her eyes were widened in anticipatory fright. "No, they're not savages. They're people, like you and me."

"Courtney said there's no law up here, and all the people live like savages and do whatever they want."

"Courtney has never been to the UP, and she should check her facts before she spews them out." My chest tightened as I realized I was defending the very place I'd denounced. When I had arrived in Chicago, the first thing I did was try to modify my speech so I wouldn't sound like I was from the UP—I stopped uttering 'holy wah' and 'eh' and most of all, I stopped waving at everyone I saw on the street as if they were an old friend. I never stopped holding doors for people, though. Holding doors was my courteous nod to humanity.

How was it that I came to be here, on this desolate highway, headed toward all that was familiar and strange?

Why was I responding to the weak, belated summons of a man who had broken my trust, disowned me, and denied Al's existence?

For Stella.

Althea: April 5, 2008

Mom clung to the steering wheel like it was a life ring and she was drowning. Her hands were shaking, but I didn't think she needed me to mention it. It wasn't until we finally cleared the long line of suburbs and finally Milwaukee that I could see farmland, and it was such a shock I think I gasped out loud. My eyes hurt from trying to stretch to the horizon, and I felt exposed and vulnerable, like a bug crossing a sidewalk and hoping a bicycle tire didn't roll my way.

"What is that awful smell?" I plugged my nose, but the stench still infiltrated my nostrils. It didn't make me gag, but it made my eyes water.

"That's a dead skunk!" Mom said. "Oh my gosh, you have probably never smelled one before!"

"I have too! We have skunks in Chicago. But not like this. This is especially fresh. Are you actually excited by this stench?" There it was—the gag reflex took a moment to kick in.

"No." She laughed. "I can't believe you've never smelled a skunk before. Whole platoons of skunks used to patrol our neighborhood at night. Once, I almost stepped on one! Scared the daylights out of me." Mom shuddered.

"I can't imagine being that close to something so disgusting."

"Skunks don't harm anyone. They just smell bad. Especially when they die on the highway and rot for a few days."

I remembered Courtney's comments about the other animals in the UP. "What about wolves? And bears?"

"There are wolves and bears, but you don't see them very often. The bears are more scared of people than people are of them, and the wolves don't bother us—they have other prey. The most common animal is probably a deer. They're everywhere—along the highways, in back yards, sometimes even walking down the main street in town."

"That's cool." I tried to picture a deer walking down a city street, but it looked ridiculous in my mind, like a Christmas cartoon special. All it needed was a scarf and a shopping bag, maybe hanging from its antlers, and a pair of sunglasses perched on its nose.

Mom had remastered her driving skills on this highway, and we zoomed along at 58 miles per hour whether the speed limit was 45, 55 or 65. She said the Corolla was most comfortable at 58, whatever that meant. My eyes were starting to get used to seeing the sky stretched all the way to the edge of the world, when we'd enter yet another small town where the buildings were so close to the road they nearly smacked us in the face. Mom called them podunk towns, and I wondered if Malcolm, whose authority superseded the Oxford Dictionary, would consider 'podunk' a real word. All podunk towns had one thing in common: corner bars.

After we passed the 59th corner bar, I finally asked. "What's with the bars?"

They were all named in a matching style: Joe's Bar, Charlie's Bar, Ernie's Bar. Sometimes it appeared they were trying to be creative: Harry's Pub, Bob's Tavern, Louie's Pool Hall.

"What bars?" She glanced at me quickly, then swiveled her head back to stare at the road.

"There's, like, a bar on every corner. Is it a Wisconsin thing? Or is it like this in the UP, too?" I hoped I had more to look forward to than 397 more corner bars on this trip.

"Wisconsin is known for bars. Beer and cheese. The UP has lots of bars, too, but I think Wisconsin has more." She sounded like a tour guide, welcoming me to Podunkland.

"Weird. And why isn't anyone walking around in these little towns we're passing through?" The ragged fringe of trees along the left side of the highway tried, and failed, to hold back the wind. The clouds pushed past the sun, leaving us in shadow for a few minutes.

"Everyone has cars. It isn't like Chicago, where you have to pay to park your car. In these little towns, you can park wherever you want for free."

"Double weird!"

"I suppose it is. Although, I thought it was strange when I moved to Chicago and found out I had to pay to park. That seemed foreign to me, back then."

We were quiet for a few moments while Mom's favorite band sang about a honky tonk woman. I felt her look at me before she spoke again.

"How do you like being thirteen?"

I grinned at her. "Lame question, Mom."

"Sorry. But you gotta give me something." She smiled. "What's new in Al-Land?"

"Let's see." I counted on my fingers. "School is fine. Courtney is dandy. Life is weird."

"Weird?"

"Yes. Weird." I spoke quietly, unwilling to let her think I was upset. I didn't know what I felt, I just knew I didn't like not knowing how to feel about Fossil. "First of all, we're driving in a car on a highway. Second, we're going to meet your dad. Third, we're, like, going in blind. Anything could happen."

Mom patted my leg. "We're going in together. We'll be okay because we'll stick together. Like we always do."

The old man on the radio sang the last line of the song: *Give me, give me, give me the honky tonk blues.*

Maybe that's what I felt. The honky tonk blues.

***

When we finally crossed the border into Michigan, my eyes were exhausted from seeing so many new sights. It was worse than spending a whole day at the museum, where you mog along from exhibit to exhibit, exercising nothing but your eyes, and by the end of it, you just want to lie down and go to sleep.

By the time we entered Iron Falls, we had passed 98 corner bars, 6 dead skunks, 2 dead cats, 4 dead deer and about a million trees. The trees on that last stretch of highway were mesmerizing—there was nothing to see except the road and the trees. At least my eyes didn't have to stretch all the way to the horizon, and the green wall of trees was kind of comforting, although I wouldn't want to get out of the car and try to walk through the thick cedars and tamaracks.

The sun was sinking behind the welcome sign at the edge of town. It read, "Iron Falls—Population 313".

"Are there really only 313 people in Iron Falls?" I asked. The town itself wasn't welcoming. If Iron Falls was a person, it would hide when someone came to the door. If it was a dog, it would roll over and play dead. If it was a ghost town, it wouldn't change a thing. Because it wouldn't need to.

"That's probably a generous estimate. They must have counted summer people," said Mom.

We followed the road, which turned sharply to the right. Same sights, different street.

Mom stopped the car and put it in park, right in the middle of the street.

"That's the house where I grew up," Mom pointed out a light blue two-story house with a wrap-around porch at the end of a long driveway on our left. It looked like the perfect storybook house from TV, sporting black shutters and white trim around its windows.

"It looks nice, Mom." The yard still had last year's grass, long and floppy, formerly green. The bushes growing along the porch needed a haircut.

Mom's face was turned toward her old house, but I don't think she was seeing it, or at least not seeing what I was seeing. She paled, and I wondered if she'd turn around and drive us back to Chicago right then, without stopping.

"Are you okay?" I asked her.

She took a deep breath. "Yeah, I'm okay, Al-kins. It's just so…shocking." She paused. "I never thought I would see this again." She gazed at the house, but this time I could tell her eyes were focused. "It's the same, only not the same. Sitting here, I half-expect Stella to come running out the door."

Mom cracked her knuckles, which is weird cuz she never does that and always tells people it's bad for their knuckles whenever anyone else cracks their knuckles. If I was suddenly blind and had to identify my mother purely by sound, if I heard the sound of cracking knuckles, I would know it wasn't her. She put the car in drive, but she didn't touch the gas pedal. We crept down the street for two blocks. I think a snail passed us.

"And that," she gestured toward a house on the right, an artsy-looking square with a tidy yard, "is Aunt Stella's house." It looked friendly. It made up for some of the rudeness of Iron Falls.

"Aren't we stopping?" My eyes stayed locked on Stella's house as we floated by until I couldn't turn my head any farther.

"I'm not quite ready. We're going to make one other stop first." And that's when she wheeled the Corolla into a parking spot, its grill mere inches from the old tattered siding, and I realized we were stopping at this trip's ninety-ninth corner bar.

"Dizzy's Bar? Really?" I raised my eyebrows.

She looked at me, no room for negotiation on her face. "We're in the UP. This is what we do here."

"You left when you were fifteen. Is this really what you did?"

Mom slumped a little. "I need a few more minutes. This is better than just driving around." She addressed the wall in front of us, then lifted her chin and turned toward me again.

"Can I come in, or do I have to wait in the car?"

"Of course you can come in! It's part of your Yooper initiation program. Kind of like hazing with suds."

I followed Mom inside the bar, a cavern so dim I couldn't see at first. Three people greeted her when she walked through the door as if they'd just seen her yesterday, and she hopped onto a bar stool and ordered a whiskey sour. I stood back, suddenly uncertain. When did she start drinking whiskey sours? Or would that be whiskeys sour?

My mom wasn't an ordinary woman. She was a Yooper woman who felt comfortable on a bar stool. And I'd thought I knew her.

"Can I help you, young lady?" The bartender looked more like an old girl than a young woman, with dull skin and drab hair pulled back into a ponytail. Her chapped hands displayed yellowed nails and cheap rings, which held my attention until she opened her mouth and I gasped, unprepared for the empty spaces in her smile.

"She's with me." Mom tipped her head toward me. "Would you like a soda, Al-Chicky? Or a Shirley Temple?"

"I'll have a—a Shirley Temple," I said, still standing back from the line of stools.

"You can sit here." Mom patted the stool next to her and I climbed up. I rested my forearms on the bar, mimicking the posture of the old, white-bearded man at the other end of the bar.

"So where are you living now, Ellen?" asked the bartender. Her necklace was tattooed on. I tried not to stare.

"I'm still in Chicago. I run a hotel there. The Phoenix."

"Nice! I bet it's fun, being your own boss. Are you married?" She looked at Mom's left hand when she asked, so she already knew the answer, but I guess she was making conversation.

"No, never married. What about you, Nadine?" Mom leaned forward and smiled as she talked. She looked like she sat on that stool every day of her life.

"I married Buddy Crampton back in ninety-nine." Nadine washed glasses as she talked, dipping each one into three different sinks and then arranging them upside down on the drainboard. "Divorced him in oh-five. Got myself three kids. I work here most days, some nights. Dizzy's a good boss." She shrugged. "It could be worse. In fact, it was worse, when I was married to that dipshit."

Nadine's laugh startled me. It was metal on metal, like the first few seconds of a car crash.

Mom made some sympathetic noises, then gestured toward me. "Althea, this is my friend from school—Nadine. Nadine, this is my daughter, Althea. She just turned thirteen, and this is her first trip to the UP."

"I could tell when youse guys walked in the door, little miss hasn't been here before. Her eyes were this big." She held her hands up around her eyes to demonstrate, and her laugh made me flinch.

I couldn't help staring at Mom's friend. Were they the *same age?* The peeling scabs on her face looked like they came straight out of one of those 'Say No To Drugs' ads about meth.

"This is the first time she's been in a bar," said Mom.

"No kidding! You don't have bars in Chicago?" Nadine laughed, as if she'd said something witty. Her laugh turned into a phlegmy cough.

"They don't allow kids," I said.

"They must lose out on a lot of business." She winked and wiped off the already clean bar.

I tuned them out while I looked around. There were five people in here: the white beard at the bar, one woman two stools away from him, and a table of three. One more walked out of the bathroom and took his chair at the table, making it six other people. I noticed the white beard wore plaid flannel, and two of the guys at the table had flannel shirts too, but they didn't have beards.

It didn't smell as bad as you'd expect. The fried-food scent seemed to have levels, like the rock layers we learned about with the newest on top and the oldest, foulest one on the bottom, holding up all the others.

The ceiling had footprints on it, in a meandering trail from the front door to the back door. Along the trail there were dollar bills, ones and fives, signed by different people and tacked into place, stretching from the trail to the edges of the ceiling. There wasn't a bare inch of space on that ceiling.

The men at the table behind White Beard were playing some kind of card game, yelling at each other about what was trump and when they should have played which card. Malcolm would have called it manufactured diversion. He would have said those gentlemen should pursue a more intellectual pastime.

Suddenly I missed Malcolm and Mrs. Whitcomb and Courtney and even Homeless Hal. It seemed like we were worlds away from everything familiar. And I hadn't even packed Mom's old photo album. I longed to open the journal Malcolm had given me, and start listing all the things that were different here. Where would I even start?

Mom suddenly slammed her empty glass on the bar.

"'Nother?" Nadine was already reaching for the whiskey.

"No, thanks, Nadine. I think it's time to face the family." Mom put her hand on my shoulder. We were two single women in a bar in the wild woods of the UP and one of us had whiskey on her breath. Would I have to drive to Stella's?

"Time to face the music!" Nadine laughed again. She must have truly believed she was witty.

I slid off the bar stool and headed toward the door. I felt everyone's eyes follow me.

"Are you alright to drive, Mom?" I asked. I grinned at her in case I needed to pretend I was kidding.

She playfully batted my head and we exited Dizzy's cave.

Aunt Stella had visited us a few times over the years, always by herself, always for about two and a half days, always talking about her kids. I'd never met my cousins, Jack and Chase, the hyper squeaks and tumbling noises in the background whenever Aunt Stella called. We had her on speaker at our end, and her voice would escalate steadily until she finally exploded and yelled at the boys to "Pipe *down*!" and then we wouldn't hear a peep for about three minutes, when they would resume running around, jumping off furniture or whatever it was little boys jumped off of, but by then Stella was "at her wit's end", and our conversation ended. I imagined Stella's wit as a frayed rope, with her clinging to the end of it.

If I was ever in a coma and I came to in Stella's living room, I bet I'd know exactly where I was before I opened my eyes.

I hoped the boys were well-piped-down for our arrival.

***

Aunt Stella's house was like I'd imagined, clean but cluttered, abused by the constant whirling of the boys, furniture a little worn but in a loving way, not a neglected way. The boys shared a room so they could have a play room full of toys, and there was a guest room and of course Aunt Stella's and Uncle Mick's room. Uncle Mick worked for the power company, but he was at some kind of seminar this week. I'd never met him.

The next morning, we rode to the hospital in Aunt Stella's pick-up truck—it had four doors and a huge back seat, way more space than Roberta's Corolla. Stella wheeled the truck around like a sports car, but when she visited us in Chicago, she drove carefully on our narrow streets and only parked in spots where she could pull through. I could see why she liked the truck—it was made for roads like this, with miles of space on each side and wide, shallow ditches, and nothing but trees in every direction. She drove through deep potholes without flinching.

By the time we arrived at the hospital in Houghton, I had filled three pages in Malcolm's journal. I couldn't wait to share some of my observations with him —he's never been to the UP, and he wanted to see it through my eyes.

We'd been in the incredibly rude, unbelievably unwelcoming town of Iron Falls for an afternoon and half of a morning and we'd already seen everything. Twice. I figured out why it seemed so unwelcoming, though: Iron Falls was like a private club—you either belonged or you didn't. In order to belong, you had to be from here. All of the locals waved to each other and some of them even smiled at each other, but if an out-of-towner—what they call a person 'from away'—was around, the hands didn't wave and smiles shut off.

Iron Falls was 47% hometown hospitality, 31% unsmiling tolerance, and 22% don't-even-bother-stopping-because-we'll-run-you-out-of-town.

I couldn't believe Mom grew up here. The air was so fresh it was sweet, and you couldn't help gulping down as much as would fit in your lungs. I never believed there was such a thing as fresh air until we climbed out of the car in the UP. I wondered if anyone ever hyperventilated simply trying to overfill their lungs with this premium air.

And Mom knew everyone—odd people walking or driving past, the cashier at the grocery store (actually, it was more like a convenience store that also sold bananas and lettuce), the man dressed in raggedy coveralls with long john cuffs sticking out at his wrists, who pulled a wagon back and forth on the sidewalk. Everyone we met was either someone she knew in school or a parent of someone she knew in school. She even recognized a couple of kids because they looked like their parents, and she knew them in school. And the school was tiny! The whole entire town and a couple of nearby towns went to this one school, with kindergarten through twelfth grade all in one building, on one floor.

All of the yards looked gross, matted grayish-brown carpets decorated with the last crusts left by the snow plows. Kids' toys were the only color on some lawns, forlorn summer relics finally emerging after spending the winter buried beneath several feet of snow.

We'd walked around the entire town three times, right down the middle of the street without even thinking about traffic.

There was a dog in town called Horace who patrolled the streets and lived on the scraps people gave him. He was considered the 'town dog', and Aunt Stella said he'd been caught twice by the dog catcher who drove through here once a year or so, and they took up a collection at Dizzy's for Horace's bail and freed him from the dog jail. He was a large, friendly mutt, black and brown with a little white near his nose, and he functioned as the town greeter. His family moved away and he escaped from their car after they crossed into Wisconsin, and he trotted straight back to Iron Falls.

Horace was the only homeless person in Iron Falls —maybe in the whole UP. I pointed out that he wasn't a person, but Stella said, "don't tell him—he thinks he is."

Elle: April 5, 2008

Stella and I stopped sharing a brain when I left her behind. When we were growing up, we agreed on everything—she asked me what I thought sometimes, and I watched her form her opinion based on mine. Other times, I'd look back at her, a couple of steps behind me, to gauge her reaction so I could formulate my own opinion. Those first few months after I left home, I caught myself glancing around for her several times, seeking her guidance, her silent support, her approval.

I wondered what she did, when she looked around for me and I wasn't there.

With no direction whatsoever, I could have picked Stella's house out of a hundred houses: neat and trim, conventional yet individual, stylish and welcoming. I paused on her porch, then opened the door and let myself in.

"Mom, shouldn't we knock?" Althea stood back near the top step, her voice a near-whisper. She looked as prim as a 1950s librarian.

"We're in the UP, Al-kins. No one knocks here. If we knocked, they'd think we're either Jehovah's Witnesses or the police."

"Who are Jehovah's Witnesses? And why would the police be here?"

"Exactly. So, we just walk in." I gestured for her to follow me through the door, the scent of graham crackers and fresh laundry inviting us in. "Come on, we're letting in the cold air."

"It seems odd, leaving your door unlocked, and any old person could just walk right in. It sounds... unsafe or something."

Two blonde tornadoes whirled past us, shrieking and giggling.

"Maybe it's more unsafe inside," Althea said under her breath.

"Come in!" Stella yelled from the other room. "Jack! Chase! Sit down!"

The tornadoes had already lapped the house again, and stuttered to a stop, pausing in midair for a second above the couch before dropping onto it. Faces flushed, the boys slumped forward and looked at us from the corners of their eyes. "Hi," Jack whispered.

Althea knelt in front of them. "I'm your cousin."

She stuck out her hand to shake. "You must be Jack," she said to the taller one, "and you must be...Chase! I'm so happy to meet you guys!" She grinned at them, and they grinned back before they could control themselves. They each shook her hand, miniature executives.

"Looks like you've got two new friends," I said. "Hey, guys, I'm your Aunt Elle. You guys look like you have lots of energy."

"We're full of piss and vinegar," said Jack. He sat up straight, chest pushed out and neck stretched to look as tall as possible.

Chase punched him in the arm. "You're not supposed to say piss!"

"Neither are you." Jack punched him back.

"Boys! Both of you, stop talking," said Stella. She looked at me while she hugged Althea hello. "I forgot to warn you, this house is a war zone. It's constant chaos. It's always a little worse when Mick is gone."

I laughed and gathered her in for a hug. "I think we can handle it. In fact, it'll probably be good for us, to have such masters of distraction around to keep us from going bat-shit crazy."

"She said bat-shit crazy!" Jack shrieked and jumped up and down on the couch three times, then landed with a thud on the floor. He stood straight, arms poking skyward in a V shape like an Olympic gymnast. Chase scrambled to copy his entire routine. Althea looked at me, eyes large and questioning.

"Oops, I seem to have slipped right back into Yooper-speak. It must have happened when I crossed the bridge into Menominee."

"Don't worry about it. We don't really censor our language—the boys know what they can say and what they can't." She raised her voice for the last sentence. "And they know they will be *punished severely* if they keep pushing the limit!"

The boys collapsed into a giggly pile on the floor, no fear in evidence.

"I wish Mick was here, so you guys could meet him." She shook her head at the boys. "And, so he could pitch in and mind the boys so we could escape if we needed to!" She swatted each boy on the backside as they sprinted past.

Stella led us toward the kitchen. "Anyway, what can I get you—dinner? Coffee? Wine? Beer? Are we going to the hospital tonight?"

"We ate in Green Bay, but we could use a snack. And maybe a glass of wine. And no, I can't handle the hospital tonight. I'd rather get run over by two tow-headed tornadoes."

"Well, I can't guarantee that won't happen. Althea, would you like juice or water?"

"I'll have water, thanks." Althea followed us into the kitchen and sat at the table as if she'd been there every day of her life. "So, what's it like living up here? Can we walk around and explore a bit?"

Stella handed me a sleeve of crackers, which I arranged on a plate while she sliced some cheese. I'd never been in my sister's kitchen before, but I knew if I allowed this fact any roosting time, I'd lose my cool. *Lose my cool?* I thought. *I really have slipped back into Yooper-speak—or maybe just back in time.*

"Mostly, nothing happens, but it seems like when something does happen, everything happens." Stella shrugged. "Probably just like everywhere else. But then again, I've never lived anywhere else. And yes—we can walk a hot lap around the town. It'll tire the boys out, too."

"What do you do for fun? I didn't see any museums or movie theaters."

"This is mainly a self-entertainment place. I read a lot, and I chase two little thugs around." Stella smiled. "Have you ever seen the show *Mayberry, RFD*? It's kind of like that, even though a few decades have passed since that show was on TV."

"I think I've seen clips of it on YouTube." Althea carefully placed a slice of cheese on her cracker and ate it in one aggressive chomp.

"I guess we're smaller than Mayberry, come to think of it—we don't even have a jail or a policeman." Stella handed me a glass of wine and took a sip from her own. "So, what's the plan for tomorrow? Are we hitting the hospital first thing?"

"I suppose. Rip off the band-aid and all that." A

shallow pool of dread formed in my stomach.

"It's not going to be that bad. He was never as bad as you thought he was. And, he's changed."

"Mm hmm. Like the proverbial scorpion, Fossil Marchand is helpless against his own nature. Sadly, those around him are often victims of that nature."

"Proverbial scorpion?" Asked Althea.

"I'll take this one," said Stella. She sat down next to Althea. "Your grandfather is a scorpion, in the truest sense of the word. He's selfish and narcissistic and quite unaware of others, much like the scorpion who once needed to cross a stream. He couldn't cross it by himself, obviously, or he'd drown. So he waited until a turtle came by, and he asked the turtle if he could ride on his back until they reached the other side. The turtle wasn't stupid, so he said, 'no way—you'll sting me and I'll die!'

'I won't sting you,' said the scorpion. 'I promise.' He convinced the turtle to carry him across.

The moment they reached the other bank, the scorpion stung the turtle. He keeled over, and as he was dying, he said to the scorpion, 'you promised me you wouldn't sting!'

And the scorpion replied, 'I didn't *mean* to sting you—it's just my nature.'" Stella shrugged again. "It's a harsh view, but sadly, it's true. And the only thing we can do is remember it, accept it, and try to get along without killing ourselves."

We sat in silence for several seconds.

"Let's talk about something fun," said Althea.

"What do you think of the UP so far?" Stella asked.

"It's true about the trees, they outnumber the people." Althea looked toward the ceiling for inspiration before continuing. "And I guess once I got used to it, not locking doors would be pretty cool. But, where do people work? I didn't notice any office complexes or big buildings."

"Great question! You have spotted the number one struggle faced by every Yooper in the history of the world. Or, at least since the copper mining companies went bust. Lots of people work two or three jobs, lots of people work for themselves, building houses and things like that. What we tell ourselves," Stella paused and placed a slice of cheese on a cracker, "is that we live in our vacation homes. We live in our summer houses, all year-round." She shoved the entire cracker into her mouth and munched loudly, then chased it with wine.

"What do you miss about living here, Mom?" Althea leaned toward me.

"I'm not sure. I miss the quiet, I guess. Sometimes the constant bustle of Chicago is too intense. It's like you have to be prepared for the city every time you open your door. Oh, and the air. I'd forgotten how fresh the air is up here—in Chicago, you stop noticing the air because it never smells good, so I think your brain tends to help you focus on your other senses."

Stella stood up. "I have to wrangle the dervishes to bed. Would you like to see your digs?"

We both stood and followed Stella to the living room, where the boys were watching TV in a tangle on the couch. "They've finally run out of steam." Stella smiled. "It's my favorite time of day."

We retrieved our bags from the car and deposited them in the guest room while Stella monitored the boys' bedtime routines and tucked them into their beds. Althea prepared for bed, but I joined Stella in the kitchen again to continue our conversation.

We talked far into the quiet night, remembering, laughing, crying and forgiving.

Elle: April 6, 2008

The sun rose early, stabbing my eyes through the gap in the curtains. Stella dropped the boys off at school and pre-school, and by the time she returned I'd figured out how to work her coffee maker and Althea was showered and ready. I quickly ran a brush through my hair and highlighted my barely-open eyes with mascara and eyeliner.

I didn't feel ready, but I didn't really think I ever would.

The drive to the hospital was quiet. Every now and then Stella would comment on the passing scenery or say something about Fossil. "He looks weak," she said. And, "he's not always nice to the nurses. I apologize to them, sometimes."

When Stella parked in the hospital parking lot, my lungs suddenly felt like they were full of sawdust and

I was only able to breathe in a tiny bit of air. My ears were ringing and I had the urge to run as fast as I could, up the highest hill around, then keep on running for days and days.

I looked at Althea and I could tell she felt the same way.

"It's a good thing I didn't eat breakfast," I said. I smiled, my teeth clenched to prevent hurling up my coffee.

Stella glanced at me. "Why don't we walk around the grounds for a few minutes. Get some air, stretch our legs."

I managed to nod.

We strolled around, walking down Fairview Street and Sharon Avenue, until we came to the nature trail.

"This is where I go when I need a little break," said Stella. "We can walk for a few more minutes, so you can see part of the trail."

The trail was wide and smooth, winding gently through the forest—if I lived here, I'd walk on this trail every day. Spring was just starting to discover the UP, and the sun felt warm on my head, and it tricked my body into feeling less anxious.

The sawdust even disappeared from my lungs. Almost.

We trekked back toward the hospital and followed Stella to the elevator, then past the nurses' station and around the corner. We reached his room. I'd have found it without Stella's direction if I'd simply followed the cold force emanating through his door.

It wasn't until my hand was on the door to his room that my stomach climbed into my throat and I regretted the second cup of acidic coffee I'd slammed down earlier. I took a step back from the door and stood off to the side with my hands clenched in front of me.

I couldn't trust my voice to say hello without quavering. What should I call him: Jack? Fossil? *Dad*?

I wasn't ready for this! The years somehow disappeared and wrapped up together in a mad tangle to attack me at once in a Dr.-Seuss-like colorful swirling vortex of anxiety, pain, regret, pride and, though I was loathe to admit it, hope.

Stella whispered, "it's time to give him a break." She headed into the room before I had a chance to respond.

The scene in the hospital room didn't make the list of my proudest moments.

I still recognized him after more than thirteen years of silence and distance. Of course I recognized him: his eyes were the same piercing blue of glacial ice, but he was somehow diminished by time, his rough edges slightly eroded. He looked frail, white hair spiked wildly like he was surprised, more wrinkles crowded onto his face than I had anticipated.

"Ellen," he whispered. His breath whistled a little,

like a screen door opening slowly on a hot summer day. "I knew you'd come back."

"I've never disobeyed you before." My voice had a hard edge.

"Hi, Dad," said Stella, loud enough to drown out my words. She opened his curtains. "You're missing a great spring day—the sun is shining, the kids aren't whining, birds are singing, hammers are swinging."

Fossil kept staring at me even as he answered Stella in his whisper-whistle voice. "I've had my day in the sun. This old hammer might be done." He winked and grinned his one-sided grin, his teeth a dark white or light gray, depending how the light hit them.

"I brought you a book to read." Stella pulled a copy of *Superior Sacrifices* from her purse. "It takes place in Iron Falls. I'm going to run down to the vending machine and grab a soda for you."

"Ginger ale," said Fossil, as Stella left the room.

I cleared my throat and took a deep, shaky breath. "It's been a while, hasn't it? You look good." I grabbed Althea's arm and propelled her toward the bed, which she'd been avoiding as long as she could. "This is Althea."

"Howdy, Althea," said Fossil, and I thought of the petrified forest Althea had recently learned about in school and how the wood had turned to stone and I wondered how long it would take Fossil to turn to stone, or if he already had. Maybe I was looking at a wrinkled old stone, and not a man at all.

Althea stuck out her hand to shake, clearly unable to imagine embracing a wrinkled old stone. "Hello, Sir." Such courage! I was proud of her grace, her aplomb, her courtesy. Her unwillingness to conduct herself on his level.

I felt like we had fallen into some sort of chasm, some crack in the world that others couldn't see, and we were trapped in Yooperland, doomed to repeat a strange and crazy loop forever after. An Alice in Wonderland alternate dimension.

He shook her hand, a more comfortable way of greeting for him than a hug. That hadn't changed. I couldn't look away from his eyes, now the color of Lake Michigan on a sunny day in August. The power held in those eyes had caused me to grow up too fast and run away too soon. And stay away too long.

I didn't look away. I wouldn't.

"You look just like your mother did when she was your age." Fossil nodded at Althea.

His simple words, innocuous on the surface, tipped my emotional scale from barely functional to fully irate. The unfairness of the past washed over me molten hot, and I welcomed the old rage.

"Please don't do that." My voice was quiet and full of force.

Fossil moved his eyes from her face to mine. "Do what?"

"Act like nothing happened." I took a deep breath. I had no idea what I would say. "How dare you summon me here, after all these years, after disowning me, dismissing Althea, kicking us to the curb like so much garbage, and then tell Althea she looks just like me, as if nothing…happened." My face was bright red and I allowed the lone tear on my cheek to fall unchecked, hoping it didn't make me look weak. My body vibrated like a tuning fork.

"You don't know what it was like, raising the two of you girls." Fossil stared hard at his toes. "I did the best I could without your mother. I made sure you were washed and fed, which is more than she ever did, anyway."

"I'm not talking about raising us, *Dad*." I poured twenty-eight years of sass into that one word.

Althea squeezed my forearm but I barely noticed.

"I'm talking about a scared teenaged girl. Fifteen years old. I'm talking about living without a safety net, at fifteen. Abandoned by my mother. Cast out by my father." My voice sounded strong and sure.

"You listen to me." He pointed his crooked index finger at me, a figurative stabbing. His rasp turned into a jagged approximation of his former voice.

I worried someone would hear us from the hallway, but I didn't dare turn my head away from him.

"You had to take responsibility for your actions." He swallowed and raised his chin an inch or two. "That's the way the world works. I took responsibility for you girls for all those years, and I couldn't take on another young one." He shook his head. "That was not going to happen."

"So you put your time in, is that it?" The tear had dried on my cheek. I felt the chilly line it left behind. I shivered.

"Look." He finally faced me, and I thought he flinched just a little when he saw the flames in my eyes. I hoped he felt the burn. "I did the best I could at the time. I didn't know what to do when your mother left, and I didn't know what to do when you got...pregnant. I couldn't even imagine you letting a boy do...that...to you." He spoke so haltingly, it was almost hard to follow. His gaze had wandered again, and he appeared to be studying the far corner of the room. "I did my best."

"Well, that seems to be the theme of the day." I took a deep breath and let it out slowly. "Now, you listen to me." My voice had somehow leveled out—I hoped I could maintain this sturdy tenor. Later, I would realize my stutter was absent, and I'd be grateful for that. "I can fix a toilet, wire an outlet, replace a water heater element, and install a level shelf."

"Ellen—"

"I'm not finished. I can cook dinner for twelve, sew a dress, plan an event for fifty, and take out the garbage."

We stared at each other for five seconds. I may

have heard an ant tiptoe across the floor.

"You weren't there when I needed you, and now I no longer need you." Perhaps it was my imagination, but I thought I saw his face fall a micro-millimeter.

"Ellen, what's wrong with you?" Stella stood in the doorway, ginger ale in hand. She took two giant steps to reach the bed and tried to put herself between me and Fossil, but I wouldn't budge and Fossil's bed wheels were locked, so she had to settle for standing on my right, practically glued to my side.

"Nothing's wrong. He called, I came running. Now I'm here."

"I'm—I'm sorry, Ellen," Fossil whispered. His whisper sounded like sand paper on rusty metal.

My ears rang in the silence. I'd just witnessed the only apology Fossil had ever issued. Not only had I witnessed it—I was the recipient of said apology.

"Well." I looked at him, really studied him, then I said, "I'm sorry, too. I'm sorry I came back. I thought I owed you something, some kind of biological debt, but I don't."

My hands were on my hips, elbows jutted, and I struggled to control the power and volume of my voice. "I survived. I succeeded. Not because of you, but in spite of you." I stepped back, still facing the bed, then grabbed Athea's arm and turned toward the door. As I opened the door, I twisted to look at Fossil one last time. "You'll never know how much you lost."

We slipped through the door, leaving Stella and Fossil behind.

Althea was the color of birch bark. I wrapped my arm around her and steered her down the hallway, away from his poisonous reach.

After thirteen and a half years of silence, Fossil's forgiveness had been flimsy and weak, a half-hearted implication. But what had I expected? A forthright, heartfelt soliloquy of love and absolution?

No. I knew better than to expect any such humanity from Fossil.

I flashed back to an afternoon when Fossil himself had taken care of me—not Heather, not Nancy, but Fossil, in person. Debilitating menstrual cramps had forced me from class. I slouched down to the school office, dizzy and disoriented, and Mrs. Parker, the painfully efficient secretary, insisted on driving me home. She even kept up a lilting monologue during the ride about the plight of women and how we are all stronger than men, and able to do more on our own than ever before. If I'd felt better, she might have motivated me to write a book or start a company. Mrs. Parker also called Fossil, who met me at home and tucked me into bed. He returned three minutes later with a hot water bottle and a hot cup of tea, and asked me where my book was so he could retrieve it. He said something about my mother then, and how her cramps had always been terrible and he'd taken care of her. The dizziness and disorientation combined with his empathy made the entire afternoon seem like a dream, a scene observed from afar through a gauzy curtain, a movie I'd viewed long ago.

I knew humanity dwelled within Fossil's tiny nugget of a heart—I'd witnessed it myself.

Althea's color gradually improved as she took deep breaths of the sweet air. My chest felt hollow, scraped out with a dull chisel, my body capable only of shallow breaths and faint heartbeat. My hearing slowly returned to normal, birdsong in the parking lot coming into auditory focus and replacing the far-away voices of the people next to me. I wondered when Stella had caught up to us.

Stella broke the silence in the truck. "Way to kick him when he's down. I hope you feel better."

"No comment." I waved her away.

I didn't possess enough energy to defend my actions, and I couldn't muster an apology for them, either.

***

We were sitting at Stella's kitchen table, chatting and drinking wine after the kids were tucked into their beds. Her face was suddenly serious.

"Don't say it," I said.

"Say what?"

"Anything about my behavior today. I waited a long time to say those things, and I'm glad I got them out." I spoke to the table. It was easier than facing my sister.

"Well, I don't think it helped his healing process any."

For five minutes, the only sound was the clock ticking on the wall.

"How about we talk about something else?" Stella said.

"Okay," I said. "I have something to tell you, and I'm just going to say it straight out."

"Okay…shoot."

I reached for the wine bottle. "Let's top off our glasses first." I poured pinot noir into our glasses, making sure we had equal levels. "I've been working on an essay for one of my classes about park design and landscaping."

"How is that related to hotel management—or did you switch majors?" Stella grabbed a pen and drew concentric circles on a napkin while she talked.

"We're learning about designing and maintaining attractive, welcoming grounds to welcome guests. But that's not what's interesting."

She stopped drawing and looked at me, waiting.

"What's interesting is, I chose a park in Minneapolis to write about because it features various storybook characters and it's being recognized for its 'gracious space', as quoted in the Star Tribune. In Minneapolis." I sipped my wine. I felt oddly calm.

She resumed drawing. "You lost me. Why is that interesting?"

"The park designer's name…is Elyse Elizabeth Nussbaum Marchand Weinhauser." I nearly choked on the words.

Stella's eyes grew wide as I finished talking. "Oh. Wow."

"She didn't design the entire thing," I added. "She was the main financial contributor—apparently she's married to some sort of lawyer or business mogul—but she provided the theme, and she worked closely with the designers, the landscapers and even the gardeners. She oversees the maintenance and approves new plantings."

We stared at each other for a minute, or a month.

"What are you going to do?" Stella asked.

I shrugged. "I don't know—I got an A on the paper."

"No, I mean—should we call her?" Stella held up her hands to support the question. "Or go see her park? Or—I don't know—visit her?"

When had Stella become so brave? She had always hidden behind me when we were kids, my ever-present shadow. *I should be the brave one,* I thought, *I'm the one who left home early—way too early—and set out on my own and raised a daughter on my own. Why am I scared all the time when I'm up here?*

"I wonder how she'd react to hearing from us." I sipped my wine and tried to retrieve a Mom-memory. "I don't know if I have anything to say to her. To—Mom. What do you say to a woman who abandoned her children? Especially if you're the children?"

Stella shrugged. "She's our mother—I'm sure we'll think of something to say." She shook her head. "I can't believe she's out there. Not that far away. Alive and walking around without us, without us knowing."

"Walking around in her park with other people's children."

Stella inhaled sharply. "She doesn't even know she has grandkids! Or, maybe she does—if she reads the papers and watches for birth announcements—but she's never met them."

I spoke gently. "Kind of like Fossil never met Al?"

"Oh. Yes, just like that." Stella folded her hands tightly. "We should go see her."

"I didn't tell you this so we could go see her. " I paused. "We thought she was dead, Stella. Do you realize how much she wrecked our childhoods?" I felt tears flutter my chest. I cleared my throat to continue. "She left us, she left Fossil, and she never came back."

"Maybe she did." Stella smoothed out her napkin, which she had been twisting into a tight pencil-sized roll. "She contacted Ariel's mom all those years ago, maybe she still talks to a few people in town. Maybe she's driven through town, or...or maybe she's even attended Althea's school plays or something. You wouldn't notice her, in the crowds you have down there."

I shook my head. "No. She hasn't given us a second thought. I don't know if we even rated a first thought. She's clearly moved on. She's busy with her money and her park and her newspaper interviews." I sounded as bitter as I felt. "And it's creepy to think she's *stalking* us. It's still hard to imagine her alive, after being so convinced she was dead, and of course we haven't seen any evidence of either."

"I've been wondering if we *wanted* to believe she was dead. When we were little, I mean."

"What?"

"I was trying to remember how everything happened, how we concluded that she was dead. Did we assume? Or did someone actually say, 'your mother died'?" She took the tiniest sip of wine.

"We were toddlers. Did we even know about death?"

"I don't know. Jack and Chase know about death, because we lost our dog last summer, and one of Jack's classmates' grandparents died last month."

"I don't remember learning about death, or how we heard Mom had died. Although," I held up one finger as a dim memory started to take on substance in my mind. "I remember Mrs.—what's her name, with the long nose and the glasses on a chain? She always had her hair in a bun, which made her nose look bigger."

"Carter. Mrs. Carter. She worked in the lunch room at school. She died last year."

"Yes, Mrs. Carter. She was there, at our house, the first day Mom was gone. And someone said, 'she was always too much for this town—she's probably in a better place now,' and I turned to Mrs. Carter, who was talking to one of the teachers, and I tugged on her skirt and said, 'what does it mean when someone's in a better place?' and she looked me in the eye and said, 'it means they're dead'."

"Oh, I vaguely recall that! I think you looked at me and said, 'Mommy isn't coming back, but don't worry, I'm going to take care of you.' And I thought to myself, 'I'll quit talking, and then Mommy will come back'."

"That was my first task, talking for you. We were quite a team. Even Fossil wasn't so bad, in the early years."

"He hired Heather, and she was lots of fun. She was like a big sister to us!"

"Do you ever see Heather? Or Nancy?"

"Heather met a fantastic guy—a dentist, I think—and moved to Marquette. Far as I know, she's still over the moon and has two or three kids. Nancy is retired, still lives here, but she's on vacation right now in Arizona."

We sat silent for a few minutes, each lost in our

own recollections.

"Do you really think we wanted to believe Mom was dead?" I asked.

Stella shrugged. "I think it might have been easier for us to think she'd died rather than think she'd abandoned us. Knowing your own mother didn't want you any more, and had left you behind, would crush any child." She spoke slowly, gravely. "I think Fossil let us believe it, or maybe even encouraged us to believe it, so we wouldn't think there was a chance she'd return someday."

"That's twisted."

"Not really. Think about it—think about the constant cycles of hope we would have been subjected to, always watching for her, wondering if she'd show up at different events, wondering if we'd hear her voice every time we answered the phone, wondering if she had other kids with another husband someplace."

"That's what I've done since I left home—watched and waited for Dad to show up. Many times I thought I saw him, but of course when the person turned around or whatever, it was never him. It was torturous."

"Fossil spared us that." She whispered. Tears were forming in her eyes, but she wasn't going to let them fall.

I cleared my throat. "Okay, so what, exactly, are we going to do? Invite her out for tea?"

"Something like that. I was thinking we could meet her someplace neutral, like a restaurant or something, and just…visit."

"What will we even talk about?"

"I guess my curiosity outweighs my resentment. If Mom won't talk about the past and is only willing to talk about today, I'll take it. But I'm going to ask her about the last two decades, and I'm going to tell her about what we've been through."

"Wow, we really won the parent lottery, didn't we? Mom abandoned us, Dad disowned me. Do we really owe either of them anything?"

"Well…I don't want to see her to assuage *her* guilt." She tapped her index finger on the table. "That is *not* my goal. I hope she has buckets of guilt, so much she can barely carry it around. I guess I need to assure myself we're not descended from some kind of freakishly uncaring robot person." She picked up her wine glass. "I'm curious. Aren't you?" She took a sip and set the glass down again.

"Never mind that we are descended from Fossil—a freakishly uncaring robot person." I saw Stella tense up and knew I should stop insulting Fossil. "Okay, so we're not meeting her for her, we're meeting her for us." I took a sip of wine, then another. "I *do* hate loose ends. I suppose this is another case of avoiding regret by facing her and finding out what kind of person she is."

Stella smiled at me and nodded.

"Okay, I'm in." I smiled back at her. "But I'm not going to tell you about any of my other classes."

June 6, 1998

Small-town graduation ceremonies are the official opening ceremonies of summer. Family reunions are planned around them. Weddings are planned around them. Even funerals, when the deceased passed during the dark, brutal winter months, might be held the same weekend as the local high school graduation, so guests can stack their events into one trip.

The woman entered the gymnasium and found a seat near the back left corner of the rows of folding chairs. She wore a plain brown dress, her hair full and loose around her face as she studied the printed program the pimply-faced boy had handed her at the door. He'd looked uncomfortable in his blazer, which he'd likely been required to wear to match the rest of the band members.

She opened the program—a single piece of paper folded in half to create a four-page pamphlet—and ran a finger down the roster of graduating seniors. The glasses she wore were mere stage props, and she lifted them out of the way to re-read the list. After checking the list a third time, she risked a quick glance around to see if she recognized anyone.

There were twenty graduating seniors today, and she'd expected to see two specific names on the roster. Only one of the names appeared there. She felt suddenly restless, and rummaged in her purse for a distraction. All she could find was a piece of gum, which she gratefully chewed.

The audio system emitted squeaks and grunts and the occasional piercing feedback, causing a mass-flinch reaction. The principal spoke first, the only one in the room comfortable in a suit, followed by the salutatorian and valedictorian and a promising elementary student who yearned to study stage acting. Another elementary student sang a jazzy rendition of Somewhere Over the Rainbow.

By now the audience members were shifting in their seats. Why did small high schools feel they had to pad their ceremonies so much? What would have been wrong with a twenty-minute presentation?

The principal finally resumed the stage and

adjusted the microphone amid squeaks and feedback, the tortured audience now clasping hands on their ears as they crossed and re-crossed legs, seeking a comfortable position on the unforgiving chairs.

He pronounced each name slowly and clearly, each child receiving a diploma, a handshake and an encouraging remark before he turned his attention to the next one.

The name she'd been waiting for was called near the middle, and she nearly stood up, she was so proud. She clapped her hands together once before she could stop herself, but the nearby infant covered her mini-outburst with its fussing and whining. Her chest filled with love until she thought she'd burst, and she realized the girl's father was standing alone in the front row of the audience. He nodded toward the freshly diploma'd girl and she pumped one fist in the air, a short jab, and grinned widely at him.

The woman suddenly felt more alone than she'd ever felt in her life. Alone and trapped, because if she left now, the chances of someone recognizing her were too great to risk.

She slumped and bent her head down, studying the seam between two pieces of flooring. She wondered again why the other name wasn't printed on the program.

When she filed out with the crowd and into the glaring sunshine, she pulled her sweater close against the cool summer day.

She left with more questions than she'd had when she arrived.

Elle: April 7, 2008

The morning arrived too early, the sun once again piercing my dreams through the curtain gap. My head was thick with the previous night's wine and revelations, my legs heavy with reluctance to see Jack again. Althea was already up, sitting in the kitchen with Stella.

"Aunt Stella's teaching me how to drink coffee." Althea smiled and held up her cup, as if toasting my entrance.

"I can't believe a child of yours has reached the advanced age of thirteen without developing a taste for the bean," said Stella. She poured me a cup and slid it into my hands as I sank down across from Althea.

"I never thought of that, but you're right, I started drinking coffee when I was ten." Í shook my head. "Who lets their kid drink coffee when they're ten?"

"Fossil." Stella shrugged. "You slept in—I already took the boys to school. Oh, and Mrs. Whitcomb called —she said Malcolm fell down the front stairs at your building, and broke his ankle. She said you shouldn't rush home, but you should know he'll be needing extra help when he gets out of the hospital."

Althea and I gasped in concert during Stella's announcement.

"When can we leave, Mom?" Her voice edged on panic.

"We'll leave tomorrow."

"I thought you were staying for two more nights," said Stella, eyebrows raised.

"I think one more night will be plenty."

"I'm worried about Malcolm. He's going to need us to help him," said Althea.

"It's not that bad, is it?" Stella looked at me. "Dad talked to you yesterday. Even though you were rude to him."

"Yes, we talked. I guess I don't know what I expected, but some kind of acknowledgement would have been nice. Maybe a hint of an apology, or a whiff of regret or sorrow or some meager request for redemption." I cradled my coffee cup in both hands, enjoying the heat against my palms and fingers. "We'll never get back to where we were before."

"He said he was sorry."

"I guess that should be enough." I smiled to

temper my words.

"You two were best friends when we were little."

"I think that's why it was so devastating when he disowned me. I always thought he was the one constant in my life."

"Hell, I only got to tag along because I wouldn't leave your side. Even with me at your hip 24/7, you two had your secret jokes and code words."

"You and I spoke in code at times, too," I said.

"Yes, we did. That was one of my favorite things about being your sister. No one else had secret codes."

"That's cool—like what was the code?" Althea asked, sipping her milky coffee blend.

"Well, we had a couple of things," said Stella. "First, there was ob-ish language. It's along the lines of Pig Latin, but slightly different. You simply insert the syllable 'ob' before every vowel you hear. Silent vowels don't count—it's more of a verbal language than a written one. So, your name, Althea Marchand, becomes ob-Al-thob-ee-ob-ah Mob-ar-chob-and." She said it quickly, smoothly, as if she hadn't stopped speaking it for the past thirteen years.

"Whoa! That sounds cool." Althea grinned, then tried her own halting pronunciation. "Mob-al-cob-olm Wob-eb-stob-er. Fob-oss-ob-il. That's fun! I can't wait to tell Malcolm about this. What else did you guys say for codes?"

"Oh, just nonsense words we'd make up to mean

our mom or something, when we didn't want others to know what or who we were talking about," I said. "We called Fossil Anti sometimes, short for Antique. Everyone thought we were talking about an aunt, so it was doubly confusing."

"What were some code words you had with your dad?" Althea asked.

"Those codes were used to point out funny things other people said or did, without letting them know we were talking about them," I said. "One of our words was Egbert, and one time we walked into a funeral luncheon at the bar, right after the funeral for old Rabbit Howser. Rabbit's son, Weasel, was greeting everyone. He was so drunk he was swaying, his shirt was buttoned wrong, and he was dribbling beer down his legs and all over his shoes. Dad shook his hand and said, 'I'm here to see Egbert.' I nearly lost it—we were supposed to be serious, or at least laughing *with* Rabbit's family, not *at* them."

Althea laughed. "What did you say?" She pushed her coffee cup away, and Stella reached over and grabbed it, gesturing for a refill. Althea shook her head no.

"I said, 'I think I see him'. Dad actually patted me on the head that day."

"He patted me on the shoulder." Stella sounded almost surprised. "I'd forgotten about that." She stopped wiping the table for a moment and stood there, remembering. "He was never a hugger, but we did get the occasional pat." She resumed wiping the table and rinsed out the washcloth.

"Another one was grease. We said 'grease it' all the time, which meant fix it, pay for it, finish it—basically, solve whatever it was. He'd say, 'you got your homework greased yet?' Or I'd say 'I greased the dishes'. People always looked at us like we were crazy."

"We got those looks all the time! I didn't know we even had to say anything to earn those looks!" Stella laughed.

"Grease it." Althea thumped her fist on the table. "Let's grease this coffee, then drive up and grease old Fossil himself." We all laughed together, and I couldn't help reaching out to muss Althea's hair, even though I know she hated it and she would spend the next twenty minutes ensuring her part was perfectly straight.

***

As we approached the hospital room, Stella fixed me in her stern gaze.

I whispered, "I'll be good, I promise."

She squeezed my hand and pushed the door open.

Fossil sat a little more upright, and his voice had returned to a weakly gruff approximation of his former rasp.

I forced a smile.

"You again." He chuckled at his own wit, and gestured for me to sit in the chair next to this bed.

I perched on the edge of it, unwilling to let him provide me with any comfort. Then I realized my discomfort wouldn't affect him at all, and I relaxed a notch and a half.

"How are you feeling today?" I still couldn't bring myself to call him Dad or Fossil.

He stuck his hand out and wavered it back and forth in a 'so-so' gesture.

"You look like some of your color is returning," said Stella. She waited until Althea had entered the room, then shut the door. "It's loud out there today. Lots of people rushing around."

"And they're all wearing squeaky shoes," said Althea. "Why would anyone do that?"

"To keep us inmates awake," said Fossil. "They talk about the healing properties of sleep, then they do everything in their power to prevent it. It's all part of their mission to keep the beds full."

"Malcolm broke his ankle," said Althea. "He fell down the front stairs at our building."

"Who the hell is Malcolm?" Fossil asked. He was in friendly curmudgeon mode today, affecting grouchy expressions that belied his sparkling eyes.

"He's our downstairs neighbor, the one with the library in his living room. It's in his dining room, too. That's where I catalog the books and create their Dewey

Decimal stickers and catalog cards."

"You work for this Malcolm?" Fossil sounded genuinely interested.

"Yep, most days after school, I go to Mrs. Whitcomb's—she's our upstairs neighbor—and help her with her cleaning chores, then I go to Malcolm's and help him enter the books he's received into his library. Mrs. Whitcomb is really nice and a great cook, and Malcolm is super smart and always says interesting things."

I wondered what Althea thought of Fossil, and if she had mentally compared him to Malcolm, who, for most purposes, more than adequately fulfilled the need for a grandfatherly figure, whereas Fossil never would. He couldn't start this late, with a teenaged girl, and expect to develop an honest relationship. And I didn't want him to.

"It sounds like you hang out in a geriatric facility," said Fossil. He waved his hand dismissively.

I'd been mistaken before: there was nothing friendly about his curmudgeonly attitude. He was treating us to the full experience.

Althea looked confused. "They're our family," she whispered.

I put my hand on her shoulder.

"They've been our family for thirteen years." My voice carried a hard edge.

Unaffected by our words, he looked at Stella.

"Have they told you when they'll let me leave this place yet?"

"No. I was hoping they told you something. Has the doctor done his rounds yet this morning?"

I stared at Stella, surprised she'd let him carry on as if Althea and I hadn't spoken.

"He should be here soon," Fossil said. He glanced out the window, away from all of us. "I'll corner him then. I've served enough time, dammit. It's time they let me out on parole."

"It can't be that bad. You have attractive nurses who answer your every call and feed you three times a day. Once you're home, you'll have to wait until an assistant is there to help you do anything. And, you'll need someone to drive you to physical therapy." Stella's voice held a thread of dismay.

"I can do everything just fine," Fossil grumbled. "And I don't need anyone monitoring me, either." He looked over at Althea. "I suppose you're going to go home and monitor poor Malcolm while his ankle heals."

Althea's face flushed. "You know, you could be nicer to us." Her voice was sharp and thin, like the edge of a scalpel.

Stella practically leapt to Althea's side to steer her away from the bed. "Althea, we can't upset him."

Althea stood her ground. "Why not? Why is he allowed to disown my mom and toss us away like—like garbage or something—and we're expected to be *polite*?

I know everyone always says life isn't fair, but this is way out there. We can't even see fair from here."

"It's okay, Althea." I spoke quietly. I had no energy left for this confrontation.

"No, Mom, it isn't. It took you a long time to stop thinking about him," she pointed to Fossil, "and then when you got that phone call the other night, it all came back." She stared at me. "I could tell. That phone call ruined your whole week. And then we came up here—and he isn't even *nice*? Are you *kidding* me?" Althea could no longer prevent her tears. She stepped away from Stella, took a deep breath and exited the room.

"This whole thing was a bad idea. We're heading back to Chicago." I glanced over at Fossil, who sat staring straight ahead at the blank wall across from his bed. "You are a son of a bitch. I'm sorry I brought Althea to meet you." He didn't move.

I caught up with Althea in the hallway. We clung to each other and cried, a long overdue release of pent-up resentment and anger and betrayal. The tiny sliver of hope I'd nurtured slipped away, too.

Hope could be a burden in disguise, I supposed, and this loss left us freer.

March 5, 2001

Hi Althea,

I'm sitting in the basement of The Phoenix, waiting for the dryers to finish. All of my other chores are done, so as soon as I make up the rooms on the first floor, I can go home to you. Back to the story...

I confronted Fossil the minute he got home from work that day. Boyd was right—Elyse had simply left us. She had chosen to walk out on us, her two princesses and her Prince Charming, leaving nothing but a brief note on Fossil's pillow. The note said she needed time to sort things out.

"I thought she'd return," said Fossil. He shook his head. "How many damn things could she have had to sort out? I gave her an awful nice life, but it wasn't enough."

Stella and I had heard people say she wasn't coming back, and we learned the phrase "she's no longer with us" from the casserole-bearing townspeople.

I'd never seen him look so sad and rejected, but still I

blamed Fossil for letting us believe she was dead. I blamed the townspeople for their tight-lipped busybodyness, for their collective ability to accurately predict Elyse's actions the moment she walked into the bar that long ago August night. I even blamed them for bringing casseroles and teddy bears. Who does that, when no one died?

Fossil tried to maintain our regularly scheduled programming, a phrase I borrowed from the TV when I came to view his letting us believe Elyse was dead as his purposeful brainwashing scheme. But when a hormonal thirteen-and-a-half-year-old girl discovers she was betrayed by not one, but two parents, a wildness starts to build inside. No, not a wildness—I'm being too gentle here, and I have to remember you won't read this until you're old enough. It was a rage. An all-consuming rage, pushing up from my belly to my chest, sometimes restricting my breathing, sometimes rejecting the food I ate, sometimes causing me to collapse into a muddle on the floor and cry and sob like an old woman whose last friend just died. It kept me warm.

In the tradition established by several generations of stoics, we kept on. Fossil and I barely spoke, and I didn't look at him enough to know if he even cared. Stella never left my side, and I feared she'd stop talking again. She withdrew, became quieter, stopped wearing makeup and doing her hair. Her strategy was to hide in plain sight, a half-step behind me. She worked harder at school and stopped hanging out with her friends, except Ariel, who was more my friend, so she didn't really have a choice. Now I understand what she was doing—

she was gathering strength for the next betrayal and, I'm ashamed to say, that one would be mine.

But we're not there yet.

Boyd felt awful—he must have apologized fifty times, until I finally told him we needed some rules for engagement. Rule one was: do not apologize for telling us our mother isn't dead, ever again. Rule two was: do not mention our mother in any context. He agreed to these rules, and life went on nearly as it had before, at least on the surface. It was like riding in a brand new Cadillac on a smooth road, then turning the corner and riding on a bumpy road with one broken leaf spring. It was there, but we could almost ignore it.

Poor Boyd couldn't change his facial expression, though. He looked so miserable, I felt bad for him.

I started having migraines, sometimes losing a day or two while I slept in a darkened room, Stella replacing the cool wash cloth on my forehead every thirty minutes. Every time I opened my eyes even one little slit, she was there, sitting on my bedside or in a chair she'd pulled into the bedroom.

The doctor blamed my migraines on the "acute hormonal changes" I was undergoing, but I knew they were caused by struggling to understand how someone's mother—my mother—could leave us behind without so much as a wave.

Sometime in the spring of 1995—I think it was May—Boyd came running into our house, grinning like it was 1992. I nearly grinned back at him, but caught myself and turned it into a smirk.

"I won!" He held a fistful of cards in one hand, like a

trophy. I'd never seen him so excited.

"You won what?"

Behind me, Stella whispered, "won what?"

"Tickets." He took his arm down, and fanned out the cards, which turned out to be tickets. "To the Grateful Dead concert. This will be Jerry Garcia's last concert. It will be an historical moment, and I. Will. Be. There."

I glanced at the tickets. "I didn't know you liked the Grateful Dead."

"Well, I don't listen to them really, but they are part of our culture. They have an entire following, the Dead Heads, and I get to be part of that for two nights. I won tickets to both concerts." He put his hands on his head. "I can't even believe it."

"How did you win?" Stella whispered. I almost cried, I was so encouraged by her curiosity.

"I called the radio station and answered their trivia question—what is the chemical makeup of onyx, which is silicone dioxide, everyone knows that, but I dialed in at the right time—and then they said I won, easy as that." He snapped his fingers.

"Wow, that's great, Boyd. I hope you enjoy the show, but don't come home tattooed and stoned, dressed in tie-dye, sporting a headband."

"Oh, Ellen." He waved one hand to dismiss the possibility. "I'm going mainly for the experience, and to study the Dead Head cult. I find it fascinating that so many people follow Jerry Garcia like he's some kind of oracle."

"How many tickets did you win?" Stella whispered.

"That's why I'm here! I won four tickets to each show!" He looked like he'd just told a joke and was waiting for us to get it.

"Good for you," I said, tempering my words with a small smile.

"No, good for all of us! I'm taking Ariel, and you, and Stella. We are going on a pilgrimage to see the Grateful Dead. I already called your dad, and he said as long as I was the one in charge of this expedition, and I agreed to keep track of you two, you can go with me." He was slightly breathless and, despite myself, I felt a quiet kindling of excitement.

The concerts were on July 8 and 9, at Soldier Field.

***

We talked about the trip incessantly. I was more excited to go to downtown Chicago than I was to see some faded hippies strumming and humming, so I scoured the Internet for information about Chicago and Soldier Field and I mapped out a couple of different routes, appointing myself Boyd's official navigator for the trip. Boyd studied up on the Grateful Dead.

The Internet was still new then, so it wasn't like the research you'll be doing by the time you read this. It's already improved since 1997, so who knows what will happen in the next ten years.

Boyd and I began an ongoing dialog centered around our research.

"Did you know," he said one day in late May, "the Grateful Dead has been together since 1965?"

"Interesting." I nodded. "Did you know Chicago has two layers? There's an underground tunnel system used by delivery trucks so they don't have to deal with the city traffic, and there's an underground pedestrian tunnel system so people don't have to walk around in bad weather."

"Cool. Did you know Jerry Garcia was once in a diabetic coma for five days?"

"Hmm. Did it affect his playing at all?"

"Smart ass."

"Did you know the word Chicago means onion field in the Algonquin language?"

We could have gone on all day. Stella or Ariel usually stopped us.

Finally, July 8 arrived. By the time Boyd rolled up in his mom's Buick, we had endured nearly two months of anticipation. We left Iron Falls at 5 a.m., allowing twelve hours for an eight-hour drive. This gave us time to check into our hotel and catch the El and walk to Soldier Field. Everyone who heard about our trip warned us about the traffic we might encounter on the way there. They also reminded us not to talk to strangers.

We had a cooler full of snacks and sandwiches, and another one packed with pop and ice, funded by Fossil and prepared by Heather. Fossil had also given Boyd some gas money and paid for our two hotel rooms, a rare demonstration of generosity. I thanked him, but I was still unwilling to give him credit for acts of humanity.

The drive was a carnival on wheels—we cranked up the radio and sang to every song that came on, then turned it down during commercials and made fun of the other cars on the road, the people, the billboards, the landscape. We were comedians, hopped up on pure natural excitement.

We were not prepared for the city. None of us had ever been out of the UP, and the size of Chicago, up close and in our faces, was shocking. We couldn't see—a tall building blocked every view! And the traffic lights—every corner had a traffic light! In Iron Falls, we had one blinking light and a handful of stop signs. Traffic in the UP is controlled more by common sense than by signs and lights. Boyd's knuckles were white as he clutched the steering wheel, but he remained calm and piloted us safely to the hotel with only two or three wrong turns.

Riding the El was a little bit terrifying, and I remember being thankful I was in a group of four. As long as the four of us stuck together, I thought, we'd be okay.

If I thought there were lots of people on the El and walking the streets, I changed my opinion when we arrived at Soldier Field. There were more people here than I could have imagined, and every shape and size and decoration, too. Most people were walking around, but some were just sitting and staring. We walked past one guy talking to a dog, sitting at the dog's level. The dog would nod his head every time the guy asked the dog a question. Apparently the dog shared the guy's philosophy. I remember thinking we had landed on another planet, and it was difficult to remember what it was like at home, where you might look down the main street and not see a single solitary soul.

We kept saying, "Wow," over and over again, and laughing at the blank expressions on each others' faces.

By the time we reached our seats way up in the nosebleed section, The Band was wrapping up their set. The crowd went crazy when the Grateful Dead walked onstage, and I thought we wouldn't be able to hear the music over the roar. I was restless, still feeling outside of myself.

"I'm going to get some air!" I shouted and pantomimed until I was certain everyone understood. Boyd pointed at the seat number to remind me where to return. I gave him the thumb's up and stumbled out of the stadium and back into the Lala-land of the parking lot. At first I walked around slowly, looking at the city, feeling like a tiny speck on the head of a pin, then I found an empty chair and sat down.

And that's where I met Roy.

The admonition about talking to strangers couldn't have applied to Roy, I figured, because if anyone ever saw Roy, they'd know there was nothing to fear. His face was open and honest, and he had the friendly demeanor of someone from a small town. It's something you can't see, but you can sense it.

He sat on the ground near my feet and we talked about everything. He was from a small Wisconsin farm town, he was eighteen, he was enrolled in UW at Madison, Wisconsin for the fall but he hadn't yet declared a major. I said I was from Iron Falls, and I said I was fifteen, then wondered if I should have lied about my age.

We walked all over the parking lot and lawn, marveling at the freak show around us. I took him back to our seats, and by then we were holding hands. Boyd shot me a warning look, but I gave him a signal that everything was okay. "He's from a farm town!" I shouted two inches from Boyd's ear. This information comforted him enough to turn his attention back to the stage. People were standing on the seats, dancing around, climbing over each other. It was chaos.

When Jerry Garcia sang Althea, Roy and I studied each other's faces for the entire song. The lyrics are poetic, like many Grateful Dead songs.

Something passed between Roy and me during those moments. My hand fit his perfectly, and if I had pulled away from him, my hand would have been boneless, hanging like a wet noodle. He gave me form and substance, and he saw me and listened and cared.

Like most teenaged boys, he had a plan.

I think I knew, on some level, what would happen, but I was still so angry with Fossil, I viewed this as my chance to retaliate. I felt strong, unstoppable, determined. Rebellious.

Roy knew about a dark corner on the outside of the stadium, and we made this our private space. I wondered if he'd been there before with someone else, but I didn't ask. Everything happened so quickly, it was almost over before I'd truly decided this was what I wanted to do. From our niche, the music sounded warped and off key.

It was a brief blip, a wild dance with a cute boy from a

Wisconsin farm town. I felt suddenly grown-up, and able to take on Fossil.

Roy showed up at our hotel the next morning—he hung out in the breakfast area until he saw us, then waved us over.

"Farm Town," Boyd greeted him, and the name stuck.

The five of us spent the day walking around the city, exploring the Science and Industry Museum and eating in little diners we found tucked into walls. It was Sunday, but you couldn't tell—Chicago doesn't slow down. The city had energy to spare, and we fed off of it, running at full speed all day, crossing streets (we'd never seen a pedestrian traffic light before) and marching along the sidewalk with the crowd. I couldn't remember the feeling of being the only person in sight, and in my mind, Iron Falls seemed lonely and desolate.

The second concert was much like the first, only Jerry Garcia seemed even more tired out and fading even faster than he was the day before, and at one point he cried for a little while. There were hundreds of popped balloons all over the ground, adding to the dead carnival atmosphere. It seemed like the show was over before it was over.

By now, Boyd was used to Farm Town and me leaving the group for a while and returning with, I'm sure, a different, private energy of our own. I didn't think Boyd or the girls knew what we'd done; they stayed in their concert seats the entire time, soaking up the atmosphere and breathing the tainted air. I didn't see the charm of Jerry Garcia—he seemed old and tired, any charisma he'd once possessed weak and fading. I did shed a tear, though, when I heard about his death exactly one month after his last concert.

I even feel a little teary now, remembering all of this old stuff. The dryers just dinged. I'll add more to this story soon.

Althea: April 7, 2008

I will stop thinking about him now.

I've written thirty pages in the journal from Malcolm—three pages of lists! I loved lists. I made a list of things I tolerate, just like in my last notebook, because Mrs. Percival said if we want to reach our goals, we first have to figure out what we're tolerating and either resolve them or learn how to deal with them. Since I'm tolerating more than ever before, I figured it's time to write it down because there are too many to keep track of in my head now.

How many other kids tolerated having a grandpa they just met and aren't sure they like, and tolerated having a grandpa-like person in their life who isn't even related to them? Probably one: me.

But I'm not thinking about him.

I also made a list of my friends, but it's a short list and it contains more names of antique people than people my age. Courtney is on the list, and Stella, and Malcolm and

Mrs. Whitcomb. I added a couple of other names of girls at school, partly to make myself feel more normal, but also because they smiled and asked me how I was doing on more than one occasion, which might mean they want to be my friend, or at least they don't think I'm invisible.

The drive home seemed shorter than it did when we first headed north, like someone stretched the road out when we left Chicago and then let it go once we reached the UP, and it snapped back to its regular length like an elastic waistband.

"How's it going, Mom? Are you glad we went on this road trip?"

"It's good." She glanced at me, then looked back at the road. "Yeah, I'm glad we went." She nodded to herself.

We drove past a huge pink mattress on my side of the road. A few yards beyond the mattress, we passed a night stand, then a dresser, lying on its back.

"An entire bedroom suite!" Mom said. "Can you imagine losing that going down the highway?"

"The only thing worse would be not noticing it," I said. "Then wondering what happened when you get home and there's no furniture. I wonder if there's anything in the drawers. They're tied shut with cords."

"I saw a recliner fly from a truck bed, once," said Mom. "It tumbled down the ditch, then landed upright, right next to a tree, like it was supposed to be there. It looked like a tableau you'd see in an art museum, like it was staged for art's sake."

"Maybe Art owned the chair," I said, one eyebrow

raised like Malcolm's when he was, in his words, 'being pithy'.

Mom tipped her head to acknowledge my joke, but then her face suddenly looked serious.

"What did you think of my—of Fossil?" she asked.

"Well—he's not what I expected. I can't really picture you and Stella living with him when you were little. He doesn't seem like the fatherly type, whatever that is."

"Sometimes we called him our cardboard cut-out, because he looked like a real dad, but he was stiff as a board. He was probably completely overwhelmed, especially when we started reaching the teenage years, and he just didn't know what to do. I suppose I should give him a break."

"A break? Why does he deserve a break? Even if you don't know what to do, you don't disown your own child." I felt my chest filling, and I fought to keep the tears away. Mom's life had been way harder than mine, because I never knew my dad. But she not only knew her dad, he raised her and Stella, practically by himself. It would be like me losing Mom now. I don't think I could survive it.

"I think his disappointment in me was so deep, he didn't know how to handle it." She spoke quietly. "And when you've only ever communicated with your daughter through witty comments and silly code words, it's too hard to start a real conversation. And your reputation for strength somehow gets equated with bravery in people's minds, which doesn't jive with the awful truth—that you've never told your daughters their mother isn't really dead—because how can someone so strong and brave be afraid of the reaction of two little girls?" Her voice wavered. She took a long pull on her water bottle and cleared her throat. "Since we didn't have that real conversation, there was no way to have one about my pregnancy."

I flashed back to being a little kid, when Mom told me 'if you can't say something nice, don't say anything at all'. Nothing nice came to mind. I maintained my silence.

"I think we did alright for ourselves."

"We did. I'm proud of you, Mom. You're the strongest mom I've ever met. I feel sorry for the other kids sometimes, with their weak little moms who would never steal a truck for them, or run away from everything they've ever known."

"I think Fossil was surprised when he saw us. He was probably expecting us to look like what he calls welfare ratbags—not ordinary people."

"Well, you showed him, Mom. I wouldn't mind if we never saw him again. He wasn't anything like I expected."

"What were you expecting?" She looked over at me.

"Someone like Malcolm, I guess. He doesn't go around hugging people either, but you know he likes you, and he's proud of you, and he approves of whatever you're doing, by the way he smiles and pats your shoulder or whatever. You can tell he has emotions, and it wouldn't be weird if we ever had a deep conversation, even though we usually talk about books and future plans."

"You and Malcolm discuss the future?" I could tell she

thought this was cute.

“He tells me which college to go to—Harvard—and tells me to keep building up my vocabulary so I don’t sound like a troglodyte when I get there.”

She laughed. “That sounds like Malcolm. He’s a good grandfather-figure for you. We really lucked out, moving into an apartment near his.”

“Sometimes, I wish he was my grandfather.” I said this so quietly, I didn’t know if she heard me.

“I think he would be honored to know that. I also think although we have a biological family, that doesn’t prevent us from having a chosen family, too. Sometimes you end up with an entirely different family, one of your own making, and that’s okay—sometimes they’re the best kind because they’ve been there when you needed them the most and they understand what you went through.”

We had passed through Milwaukee—I was eager to see Malcolm, to check on his ankle and hear the story of his fall. Mrs. Whitcomb was preparing a chicken pot pie for all of us, and I would help Malcolm set the table at his place so he wouldn’t have to climb the stairs with his crutches.

Elle: April 8, 2008

I wondered what, if anything, I owed Fossil. I also wondered what, if anything, he owed me. Maybe we're even. Maybe the only thing you owe your offspring is to help them survive until they can make it on their own, even if that turns out to be when they're fifteen years old. Maybe the only thing we owe our parents is respect and gratitude for raising us, and it's okay to go separate ways. Maybe the bond between parents and children that I've read about, and experienced with Althea, doesn't naturally exist between every parent and child, and in many cases, maybe it can't be forced.

It's like agreeing to disagree.

Spending so much time in a car with Althea made me want to buy my own car and take road trips—we could go to the Grand Canyon, or DisneyWorld, or the redwood forest. Or all three. How many miles did Stella and I ride in Fossil's truck when we were small enough to share a seat belt? Hundreds. Millions. He took us road hunting, country road driving, visiting, Sunday driving. I think driving was his favorite thing to do. Sometimes he'd take us to Balsam Falls, and we'd walk the path through the woods to the hidden waterfall. Only the locals knew about it—there was no sign near the road, no real parking area, just a slightly wider spot along the shoulder of the road. The path was well-traveled, but it was nearly a mile long over fallen trees and across a narrow stream, which we were able to portage by stepping on the rocks sticking out above the water.

All of my favorite childhood memories take place in Fossil's truck cab or on a woodsy trail. We were his two favorite companions, until we weren't. Stella said he was a lot nicer after I left—she assumed his sudden mood upswing was due to his fear of losing her, after he'd already lost me. But I always wondered if the underlying tension between us, and our too-similar personalities, were too much for him and he felt a kind of relief when I left. My leaving relieved him of responsibility and of facing his own imminent grandparenthood, which I'm sure he felt he wasn't old enough to experience, even though he was old enough to be my own grandfather when I was born.

Stella had said Fossil thought he was doing the

best he could by allowing us to believe Mom had died that January day. Maybe she was right—and maybe this belief spared us countless torturous moments of watching and wondering, waiting for her to reappear.

Maybe we wouldn't have recovered from abandonment as easily as we had from her death. Not that it was easy—we grieved for years—but at least we believed she'd only left us because she'd died. The one excuse no one can call flimsy.

I wondered if Mom knew we thought she'd died. This thought slammed into me with the force of a tornado, and I snapped upright in my seat. Good thing I already had two hands on the wheel. How *would* she know what we thought? But if she didn't know, why didn't she contact us during the past two decades? Maybe Fossil told her not to—she would probably obey him, because she'd feel guilty for leaving, and if he said it was best for us if we didn't know where she was, she'd probably go along with that. But she'd also know that we are adults now, no longer under Fossil's control. But I didn't know how much he'd controlled her, either. I guess most toddlers aren't familiar with the inner workings of their parents' marriage.

My mind spun with various possibilities, each one more difficult to consider than the last.

No matter how many scenarios I invented, none of them were sturdy enough to justify leaving your own daughters and never contacting them again.

I wondered what Fossil would think about our meeting Mom after all this time—would he tell us what had really happened? Did he know what had caused her to leave? Was *he* the catalyst? So many times, kids think everything is about them, when they are peripheral to the action, merely providing an added distraction or disturbance, like dangling modifiers.

"Mom? Are you okay?"

I was so deep inside my own thoughts, I'd forgotten Althea was sitting next to me in the front seat. "I'm fine, Al-bug. Just thinking about my mom, and about seeing her again and finding out what happened all those years ago."

"That's gotta be weird, knowing she's your mom but not knowing anything about her."

"It is weird, and I'm wondering how much of what I've always thought I've known about her is true. Maybe she lied about everything." I sighed. "Then again, maybe she told the truth, and Fossil didn't really lie either, per se, but he didn't bother setting us straight." I looked over at her. "Families are complicated."

"Ours isn't." She smiled. She looked comfortable, partially curled up in her seat, feet on the dashboard, hugging the journal Malcolm had given her. "Ours is simple and true, and strong and…chosen. Because we chose Malcolm and Mrs. Whitcomb, and they are more like family to us than anyone else, except maybe Aunt Stella."

"I would do well to take a page from your book, and remember that when we meet my mom, if we ever do."

"I'm sure you'll meet her." She looked at me. "What made you pick Chicago, when you left home? How come you didn't move to Green Bay or Appleton or some other town along the way?"

I thought back to my memory of that time, slightly frayed around the edges and worn from over-examination. "Well, we had just gone to the Grateful Dead concert, and I thought Chicago was the greatest city on earth. And—I've never told anyone this—but I thought Chicago was kind of like me." Althea waited. I continued. "You know, from Homeless Hal, how the city has two layers? One public, and one pretty much hidden from the casual observer's view?"

"You mean the Pedway and the underground truck delivery route?"

"Yes. Well, I always felt like Chicago and I both have our secrets. Chicago has an entire underground network and a shady past, to put it mildly, and I have secrets and a past I don't share with people until I know them really well. When I was fifteen, I saw myself as this kind of traumatized survivor of betrayal no other human had ever known, and I thought of Chicago as another kind of survivor, rising again after a major fire, thriving during Prohibition, living down its own reputation for debauchery and Mafia ties and who knows what else." I stared out the windshield, seeing what I saw as a girl of fifteen, scared and on the run. "I guess I thought a city like Chicago had room for me, because I was one of the city's own, like a displaced orphan returning to my rightful home."

"Well, I'm glad you picked Chicago. I think you're right, it's the greatest city on earth, and after visiting the UP, I'm double-glad we didn't stay up there!" Althea sat up, excited. "I would probably be wearing flannel!" She mock-shuddered, then slumped back in her seat as if she was exhausted. "Although, the fresh air was nice." She smiled.

***

When I picked up the phone to call Roberta, there was no dial tone. "Hello?"

"Wow, you're good. It didn't even ring." Joel's voice made me smile without trying.

"Mr. Jamison, I presume."

"You can call me Joel. Or late for breakfast." He laughed, and my chest grew warm. "You're a hard lady to reach."

"Yes, well, I told you I was in the UP. They just have strings and cans up there—no phones yet."

"Maybe it's time you got a smart phone."

"Ugh. Smart phones are over-rated. Al and I each have a flip phone, and they work just fine. Although, they didn't work once I crossed into the UP. We had enough signal to send and receive texts, but it was never strong enough for a real call. Stella's works, but she has a different provider." I clamped my mouth shut to prevent further verbal spewage.

"I just thought I'd call to see how your dad is doing."

"Thank you. He's fine. I probably won't be going back." *Ever*. I hadn't yet told Joel about my past, and this wasn't the time to start that Grimm fairy tale.

"Okay. It turns out I'll be back in Chicago sooner than I thought—usually I'm there every six months or so, but my company is sending me to train someone at our Chicago office. I'll be there in two weeks. So, if you're free then…"

I swallowed the butterflies and tried to sound casual. "I should be. Why don't we pencil in a date now? How about Tuesday of that week?"

"I'll take it! I'll meet you at The Phoenix. I'm not sure where I'm staying, but I know where you'll be."

"Sounds good. See you then."

"I'll wine and dine you at an authentic Italian place I found."

"Authentic Italian? In Chicago?"

"Okay, so it's not the first Italian *ristorante* to open doors in your fair city, but it has *delizioso lasagne*." He donned an Italian accent.

"*Perfetto*." I played along.

We said *ciao* at the same time and hung up the phone.

I sat down at the kitchen table and breathed in and out and thought about the phrase 'I have a date'. Almost thirty, and I had an actual date.

What would Althea think?

March 10, 2001

The ride home from Chicago in a car full of friends ranks up there as one of my favorite memories. We were four Deadheads, or temporary Deadheads at least, who'd shared a very cool experience.

How could we go back to our dreary backwater town after visiting a city as grand as Chicago? It was like eating nothing but shredded wheat all our lives, then discovering something zesty, salty, sweet and tangy—then resuming our all-shredded-wheat diet.

The car was quiet. Ariel and Stella slept most of the way, and I spent the time wondering if I'd ever see or hear from Farm Town again. Boyd concentrated on the road. The heat wave that would make national news and cause 750 deaths would hit the Chicago area in 3 days, but of course the temperature in the UP would only ascend to a tolerable summer day level.

About two weeks after the concert, I felt a bit sick in the morning. I already knew what had happened, but I had to wait until I went to Houghton to buy a pregnancy test, so no one would know I bought it. I used it in the ladies' restroom right there in the store, and sure enough, there was the first evidence of your life.

I wasn't scared, or doubtful, not even once. I want you to know that. The rage I'd tended and kept alive in my chest had morphed into power and courage, and I was certain I would be the kind of mother I'd thought I had when I was little, the kind who loved hanging out with her kids and wouldn't leave them for the world.

I didn't tell Fossil about you until the beginning of October. Predictably, he freaked out and manhandled me into his truck and drove me to the abortion clinic in Houghton. I guess all it took to break Fossil's stoic non-reaction to life's tragedies was a teenaged girl with a belly bump.

Luckily, for me and for you, the woman at the clinic was kind and understanding, and she took me into a room with a desk and three chairs, each one supporting a taller pile of books and files than the last, to discuss my intentions. I told her I intended to raise my child, and I understood I'd have no help from Fossil, and she said it was my decision—not his—whether or not I would have this abortion. "Even though you're fifteen," she said, "I won't do this procedure unless you allow it. You're clearly in control of yourself mentally and physically, and I can't in good conscience do something like this against my patient's wishes."

Those were the sweetest words I'd ever heard.

Fossil followed me out of the clinic to the truck and we sat there for a few minutes before he turned the key.

I stared straight ahead and told him what he didn't want to hear. "I aborted the abortion before they aborted."

"Well," he said, pausing to turn the key and let the truck roar into life, "looks like you're fucked."

It didn't take long to figure out what he meant: I—we—had been evicted.

The next few weeks were hardest on Stella. Fossil and I fought and screamed at each other. He called me a slut and a whore, and called you a bastard. He said neither one of us would have a snowflake's chance in hell of succeeding. I called him a liar and a no-good-rotten excuse for a dad. I said I learned everything I knew from watching him.

The ugliness spewed out of both of us and landed all over Stella.

It was a gray day in early November when I left. Everyone was in full deer season preparation mode, the town was gearing down for the coming winter, Homecoming had come and gone and the days were rapidly shortening. I loaded up Fossil's oldest truck, a battered old Chevy S-10 he kept for the grunts to drive to job sites, and headed toward Chicago. The truck was slated for the junk yard, so I told Fossil's office manager, Nancy, that I was delivering it for him. She produced the signed title, and I shimmied back into the driver's seat next to my pile of clothing and possessions. Like most Yooper kids, by the age of fifteen, I'd been driving for about a year and a half, although I didn't yet have a license, so Nancy didn't think twice about my claim.

I closed my account at the credit union, pocketing a little *over $300 I'd saved from babysitting and working for Fossil over the years, and I said goodbye to Stella. No one else knew I was leaving. "He doesn't deserve to know," I told Stella, when she asked if I'd said anything to Fossil. "It's not like he'll worry." I didn't ask her to come with me, and I've always regretted that. I should have asked her.*

As soon as the truck was on US-41 heading south, I felt the dread receding. My sense of impending doom transformed itself into excitement, anticipation, and a terrifying loneliness. I could go anywhere, do anything. Maybe I'd become an engineer and design bridges and highway interchanges, looping asphalt in graceful arcs to carry cars safely in their desired direction. My bridges would have been artistic, interesting, with a signature touch—my symbol—inserted someplace subtle, a tiny personal detail linking all of my work together. I felt like the world was welcoming me, and I had but to select my place in it. There was ample room to accommodate my dreams.

The truck was more than just an eyesore—it was also a mechanical disaster. It was a stick shift, but first gear had stopped working, so I fluttered the clutch and hopped forward in second gear every time I had to come to a complete stop, which I tried to avoid. In one of the little podunk towns that punctuated the Wisconsin farmland, I lost second gear and had to start out in third gear. I worried the erratic jumpy rhythm would draw the attention of a policeman, but luckily I didn't see any.

The failing transmission kept me busy, but somehow worry

crept in through the cracks of my mind—worry about where I would sleep that night, worry about what would happen to us, worry if I'd made an unfixable mistake. In my mind, there were already two of us, and we were a team. A formidable team of two, stronger than any other team anywhere.

Every mile I drove carried me farther from what I'd always known, and my mind started churning in circles of ever-increasing doubt. How would I support myself? I didn't even have a driver's license! How would I apply for a job where no one knew me? And what would I do with this stupid truck when it failed for the last time? A gauzy fear crept in from the edges of my mind, choking off my excitement, blanketing my anticipation in a king-sized certainty that I'd made the biggest mistake of my life.

This emotional teeter-totter continued for hours, lifting me up and slamming me back down.

By now, Fossil must have heard that I'd left, which meant I no longer had the option of returning. Fossil firmly believed in lying in the bed one created, and I knew he wouldn't rescue me unless I was somehow in mortal danger. Even then, there was no guarantee.

I'd abandoned my college plans, and rejected any help Fossil might have given me, by leaving home.

Although I had no real destination in mind, I realized I was driving toward Soldier Field. Even as I knew I'd never make it that far, I stayed on Highway 41 until I drove into the neighborhood where we live now.

When the truck rolled to its final stop, I was three blocks off

Highway 41, rigid with fear and thankful I'd nearly run out of gas instead of letting the truck die with a full tank. I took a few deep breaths and looked around. I'd pulled into a weedy gravel parking lot next to an abandoned building. Two kids walked by, one of them tugging a cocker spaniel on a leash, the other whistling and carrying a baseball glove. The air didn't smell as fresh as it did at home, but it smelled like possibility to me. If I hadn't been merely fifteen, I probably would have bought a bus ticket home, but I was young and dumb enough to believe I could make the best out of any situation.

I brushed my hair into a pony tail and added some mascara and lip stick to my tired face. It was the only make-up I had, and I hoped it drew attention away from, rather than toward, the weariness I could see in my reflection.

The neighborhood was pleasant—brownstones and trees, late model cars parked along the sides of the street. I was close to an intersection, so I turned off Cottage Street onto Hale Street and walked until I came upon The Phoenix Hotel, A Friendly Luxury Boutique. A discreet sign in the window said Help Wanted. I walked inside and an older woman wearing a light blue cotton dress and sensible shoes was dusting the bookcase. She looked up when I walked in the door, her sharp eyes assessing my appearance before I said hello.

My bladder had my full attention by the time she greeted me.

"Can I help you?" She had a musical voice and I could tell she smiled a lot.

"Yes, I—I—I'm wondering if you have a rest room." My

stutter always appeared when I was extremely nervous. It efficiently worsened the condition. "And, a—well, a job application." I added this last without thinking.

"Oh!" She clapped her hands once, somehow managing to look graceful with her dust rag. "But that's great news! The ladies' room is just around that corner." She pointed a manicured nail and smiled, her eyes never leaving my face. "Take your time. I'll put this stuff away and get an application for you."

Ruth hired me that day, and I started the next morning, cleaning rooms. I tried to picture the people who would stay at the hotel in the rooms I prepared, and I hoped someday I'd be able to afford a hotel room so I could move out of the truck.

I hope you remember Ruth. She's one of my favorite people.

I'm hunched so low over this desk, my back is starting to ache. I'm going to take you for a walk to enjoy the sunshine today. It's still cold out, but you have new boots and I know you're dying to wear them.

Althea: April 8, 2008

I dropped a bright orange hat on Homeless Hal's head. His eyes rolled toward me and he smiled. "Thanks, Peanut" he said. "I like the color."

"You're welcome. I thought you should have something that will show up, for safety, and also because it's spring and you need to show your spirit."

"Where have you been? I haven't seen you in days and days."

"Mom and I drove to the UP to visit family. Did you know there are more trees than people up there? And in Wisconsin, there's a bar on every corner. We drove past 99 bars."

"That doesn't sound right." He shook his head and wiped his nose on his crusty sleeve. "Did you know," he paused to make sure I was listening, "that Al Capone's speakeasy was on the top floor of the Carbide Building? Everyone else hid their illegal establishments in dark alleys and basements, but not Big Al. No sirree, his speakeasy was perched above the city so he could look down on everyone."

"How do you know so much about Chicago?"

He straightened and grabbed his lapels. "I'm a renaissance man. A student of life." He looked at me, and swept his arm to encompass the entire city. "Chicago is my passion."

I waved at him and crossed the street to meet Courtney to walk the rest of the way to school together.

"Well? How was it? Did you see any wolves or deer or moose?" Courtney tended to bounce as she walked, and today she seemed to be walking on new springs. Her hair was pulled back into a pony tail and her glasses were where they belonged. The only visible funkiness was a light streak of purple hair on one side of her head.

I laughed. "No, but I saw some dead skunks. And Malcolm broke his ankle, which was bad, but it made us come home early, so it was kind of good."

"Oh, poor Malcolm!" She did a little twisted ankle shuddering dance. "So, you met Grandpa Fossil?"

"I don't call him Grandpa. You wouldn't, either."

"What? Why?"

"He looked like a scarecrow with Einstein hair, only not quite that long, and his eyes look right through people."

We walked a few steps before Courtney asked, "What do you call him?"

"Nothing, really."

"What did he say?"

"I don't know, just stuff. Mom yelled at him and he

yelled back. They had the fight they never had fourteen years ago."

"Your mom yelled? No way!"

We both jumped over a puddle without breaking stride.

"Yep. I couldn't believe it, either, and I was there. I saw the whole thing."

"What did she say?"

I gave her the highlights, acting out the eye movements and jaw clenches.

"Whoa." She shook her head.

"I doubt we'll have to visit Fossil again."

"I'm sorry, Althea. I thought you'd have a grandpa after going up there."

"That's okay." I waved my hand, throwing away a grandpa. "It's not like I lost something I had. I lost something I never had, which isn't a loss."

"Well," Courtney paused for effect. "I found something of yours."

"You didn't!"

"Yep. He lives in Madison. I'll show you everything after school."

"What does he do? Does he have a family? Is he cute?"

"He's...nondescript. Two sons. I'll tell you everything after school. There's a lot."

We walked about fifteen steps in silence. My heart may have stopped beating. Or maybe my lungs collapsed.

"Did everyone have beards up there?" Courtney

asked.

"No. That's a myth. But I saw lots of flannel. And I went to the bar!"

"No way! They let you in the bar? That must be what they meant about having no laws up there. What was it like?"

I thought about this. "Dark, but nice. The ceiling was plastered with money—dollar bills stapled and taped up there, covering the whole thing."

We were approaching school, merging with other groups of students heading toward the doors.

"See you after school," she said.

"See you!" I said.

***

After school, I checked on Malcolm while Courtney went home and gathered the evidence.

"Thank you, Fledgling. I do appreciate your concern." Malcolm didn't seem to feel like I was monitoring him. I wished Fossil could learn how to behave from what he calls my geriatric ward.

When Mrs. Whitcomb showed up at Malcolm's door with an afternoon snack of pumpkin bread and tea, I excused myself to go home before Courtney got there.

She arrived five minutes later, and I buzzed her in. She brought a short stack of papers.

"Wow, for your first case, you found lots of evidence." I greeted her.

She thrust the papers at me and we walked into my

bedroom to spread everything out on the bed.

"Once I figured out which Roy Harrison it was, the rest was easy," she said. "I don't know how anyone found anyone before the internet."

"Mmm hmm." I could hear her, but I couldn't tell you what she'd said.

I worked quickly, arranging the bits and pieces Courtney had found so I could see everything all at once. We had a Google map image of his address in Madison —both a street view and a regular map view; the concert schedule from 1995, which she'd printed out at school; and three printouts of the links she found by Googling Roy Harrison Madison WI.

He was the CEO of a credit union, where he'd worked for nine years, and his professional photo showed a balding man in a suit. Judging from this picture, he had no personality whatsoever. But Courtney also found a picture of Roy Harrison at someone's wedding, and it must have been late at night because he was outside after dark, and he'd already taken his suit jacket off but he still wore his vest, his shirt sleeves rolled up sweaty arms. He held a beer like he was toasting the photographer. He had a friendly smile, but he looked like the kind of person who might wander off and stumble into the pool and no one would be surprised.

The third entry Courtney had printed was a short article about giving back to the community by building houses for Habitat For Humanity. Roy wore a tool belt and held up a hammer, but it looked like he never used a hammer and wasn't too sure how to hit a nail with it. The article said his son Dylan helped him and the rest of the volunteers build the house by keeping the job site clean and sweeping up the sawdust and picking up stray nails. Dylan was five when this article was written last summer. Roy's wife Lisa helped the Habitat project by bringing pizza to the crew at dinnertime. They also have a two-year-old named Grayson. *That must be Lisa's maiden name*, I thought. Was Dylan named for Bob Dylan? Had Roy unknowingly copied Mom's musically-influenced naming scheme?

In my notebook, I added "not knowing Roy Harrison" to my List of Tolerations. Then I added "knowing about Roy Harrison" on the next line.

On the notebook page dedicated to the Roy Harrison Project, I wrote down Roy's address, his wife's and sons' names, his email address, and his work history.

"What are you going to do with all this?" Courtney held the Habitat For Humanity article by one corner and looked at me. Her eyes bounced all over my face and I suddenly didn't know how to hold a normal expression in place.

"I don't know. I want to meet him, somehow. Or maybe I just want to see him. I don't know if I'm ready for him to know about me."

"You could go to his credit union and see him at work," she said.

"And do what? Open an account? What if he knows my mom's last name and thinks to himself, 'hmm, this must be mine and Ellen's daughter'? How will that go down, exactly?"

“Well, you could just go there and ask about opening an account. Ask them what the requirements are.”

“I doubt he opens accounts. He’s the CEO. He probably sits in his office watching TV all day.” I leaned back, crossed my feet at the ankles on my bed, and put my hands behind my head.

“You’re right. You’d have to hide behind the ficus and spy through his office window.” She laughed. “You could wear a khaki jungle outfit like that guy who always said ‘Crikey’ on that TV show.”

I sat forward. No matter what I did, I felt uncomfortable. I needed to move.

“I’ll need binoculars!” I mimed holding a pair of binoculars, craning my neck to see around the foliage.

We laughed for a minute, rocking back and forth on my bed.

“How are you going to get there?”

“I don’t know. The train?” I stood up and walked to the window, then over to the door.

“There might be a train. It probably only runs once a day or something." Courtney's eyes followed my movements. "And you’ll have to get your own ticket somehow. Are you okay?”

"Huh?" I looked at her, then down at my ever-moving feet. I flopped back onto the bed. "Yeah. Just a little… freaked."

We sat in puzzled silence.

“Well,” I finally said, “I’ll just have to watch and wait. Like Mrs. Whitcomb always says, luck is preparation meeting opportunity.”

"Are you going to email him? You've got his email address right here." She pointed at the paper.

"And say what?"

"I don't know." She shrugged. "Ooh! You could pretend you're Elle."

I nodded slowly. "Maybe I've been thinking about him lately, and I want to see him."

"Hmm. Maybe you're going to be in Madison for…work or something…and when you Googled Madison, his Habitat For Humanity article popped up and you thought to yourself, 'hey, I know that guy', so you Googled his name and found his email, and then you emailed him!"

"That's perfect. Okay, I'll do it." I opened my email server, then realized if I was posing as Elle, I'd have to open a new email account. "I'll be gratefulyoopergirl @gmail.com," I told Courtney. She scootched next to me and hovered over my shoulder as I typed. I felt her breath on my neck.

Within five minutes, I had a new email account. I clicked Compose and entered rharrison @madcitycreditunion.com, and typed "long time no see" on the subject line.

"That's good," said Courtney. "That will definitely get his attention, so he'll open the email."

"Wait a minute. I don't know when I'll be in Madison. I can't give him a date for my fake work seminar!"

"Okay, so, you'll say…umm…I'll be there soon—I don't have the dates finalized yet. That sounds just like your mom."

"Like I'm waiting for confirmation or something."

"Yes, you're waiting for your Human Resources department to book your tickets. Maybe there are several conferences, and you're not sure which dates you'll get."

I stared at the screen again, fingers hovered over the keyboard. The blank square challenged me to fill it. It taunted me. I stared it down, then started typing. I tried to channel my mother.

Hi Roy,

Imagine my surprise when your name came up

I backspaced, erasing everything except Hi Roy.

It looks like I'm going to be in your neck of the woods

I backspaced again. This was the worst writing I'd ever committed to screen.

Do you remember me? We met at the Grateful Dead concert in Chicago in 1995. Anyway, I was just researching Madison because I'm going there soon for a work conference, and your name popped up in an article, so I tracked you down.

Mom was like a kindergartener when it came to Internet research, or anything to do with technology, but Courtney reminded me, "he doesn't know that," so I kept going. Her cyber-skills were improving since she'd enrolled in college classes, but she was still mired in the last century. Or maybe the one before that. She called herself a luddite, and Malcolm agreed.

If you're not busy when I'm in town, maybe we can get together and catch up.

"You should put something like, 'take care' or 'I hope all is well'. Grown-ups always say something like that in their emails," said Courtney.

"Good idea." I typed 'I hope all is well with you,' then I signed it Ellen Marchand.

I read it once out loud, then three more times to myself, then I hit Send. And then it was gone, into the ether, traveling faster than a phone call to Roy Harrison, ex-boyfriend, CEO, husband, amateur carpenter, father of two, and father of me.

My stomach clenched. Courtney and I faced each other, our cartoon-scared faces pasted into place, and laughed again, rolling around on the bed. It felt weird to laugh, but it felt good, and there was no way I could stop it.

March 12, 2001

I lived in my truck for a week, parked in that weed-choked gravel lot, sleeping half-stretched-out across the seat, waking up when the sun crested the dashboard, showering at work in one of the rooms. The nights were long in the truck—someone walking by or a car backfiring woke me in a full panic. It was cold, too. I buried myself in layers of clothes each night. If anyone had shined a flashlight in on me, they'd have seen a pile of laundry and probably not noticed the girl cocooned within.

"Elle," Ruth said one morning when I walked through the door, "where are you living?"

"On Cottage Street," I said. Literally.

Ruth looked at me, waiting for more. "About three blocks away."

"Look, Elle," she said, as serious as I'd ever seen her, "you need to tell me what's going on. I knew the first time you walked in the door that you had a story—I can always spot a person with a story to tell—and I want to help you out, but I need you to tell me the whole story."

After one short week, Ruth was my Mary Poppins, fun but firm, always knowing the correct way to handle everything, always practical and classy, with a touch of whimsy. She could have written a book about elegance, etiquette and poise. Ruth enthralled me, and I'd already started to emulate her movements and the cadence of her voice, which seemed to set everyone at ease whenever she spoke.

But I hadn't yet tested her with my full truth. I didn't even know my full truth—was I considered a runaway? A fugitive? I'd crossed two state lines—was that a felony for which I could be tried as an adult? I'd dropped out of high school, I'd stolen a truck, I was pregnant and on the run. I couldn't bear to see Ruth's face when she learned these horrible things about me. I couldn't handle the responsibility for another massive disappointment from someone I cared about.

So far, I'd kept a tight lid on everything: my past, my worries, my mistakes, my regrets. I remember wondering: do fifteen-year-olds even have regrets? I was an overachiever in the regret department, and the rash reaction category, but I was determined to make it on my own and I was still so stubborn and naive I believed I didn't need anyone's help.

The temperature dropped each night, the truck was increasingly uncomfortable, I could no longer keep my jeans zipped, and the lid I'd screwed tight on the jar that held my anxieties developed a hairline crack and the pressure grew and grew and grew.

"Tell me when you're ready," she said. She reached out and grabbed my upper arm, her standard display of friendly

comfort. "But don't wait too long."

"I—I'll be ready—soon." I promised.

That evening, a policeman stopped by my Chevy condo.

"Good evening, Miss. Are you having car trouble?"

"Hello, Off—Officer." I squeaked. I definitely squeaked. "I think the transmission failed. I can't get it to go into first, second or third gear any more. Fourth and reverse still work, and I think I need to take it to the junk yard. But I don't know where the junk yard is, and I can't drive there in reverse." The words turned on like a spigot on a garden hose, and they sprayed everywhere like crazy.

"You have an awful lot of clothes in there. Are you moving or something?" His face showed no expression. He could have been playing poker. "I see you have Michigan plates."

"Well, yes, I'm new in town here and I just started working at The Phoenix Hotel, right over there." I gestured in the general direction and he nodded, like he knew exactly where The Phoenix was. "And I haven't had time to move everything out of the truck yet. But I also have to get it towed to the junk yard, or get it there somehow, and—"

He silenced me by holding up one finger. "Do you own this truck?"

"No, it's my father's. He was going to take it to the junk yard, but I needed a ride to Chicago, so I told him I could take care—"

Again, he held up one finger. "Okay. Let me see your license and registration, and I'll get you a couple of phone numbers for scrap metal yards that might be interested."

"Oh, thank you so much, Officer—" I searched his broad chest for a name, finally finding it among his other ribbons and patches. "Oglethorpe. Sir. Thank you, Sir." I handed him the registration and the signed title, hoping he'd forget about my driver's license. No such luck. "Where's your license?" He asked.

"I don't have it with me right now." I tried to look confident. I tried to channel Ruth, and appear poised and elegant.

"Okay, look. I think you're telling me the truth, and I know there's more to the story, but I'm going to let this one go. I'll get you the numbers for the scrap yards, and you make sure this truck disappears within 48 hours. If it's still here after 48 hours, I'll stop by The Phoenix and we'll have to get to know each other better. Sound fair?"

If I could sing, I would have sung an aria right then and there. I would have danced a jig or jumped over the moon.

"Yes, Mr. Oglethorpe, Officer, Sir. That sounds very fair to me."

He walked back to his car and I saw his partner sitting there, taking notes about something. Mr. Oglethorpe jogged back to my truck.

"We've got an emergency. I'll drop those numbers off for you when I finish work in the morning. Forty-eight hours. I'll be counting."

I yelled after him as he ran back to his patrol car, thanking him again and telling him I'd keep my promise.

That's the first time I talked to you, Al-sweetie. I rubbed my firm dome of a belly and I said, "Seed pod, that was our second big break. We are on a roll."

And I felt you move for the first time, right there in the front seat of that rusty old mechanical disaster on bald tires in a weedy gravel lot in the middle of a city that held more than one thousand times the population of Iron Falls.

I felt mighty and small at the same time.

Althea: April 11, 2008

Three days went by with no response from Roy.

Three days.

In those three days I checked my new gmail account thirty-one times. I added 'Managing email' to my list of tolerations. I chattered at Mom and smiled a lot, so she wouldn't think anything was up. I sent thirty-one texts to Courtney that said: *Nthg yt.*

And I waited.

On day four, I was wondering if I should contact Google and have them check my email account to make sure it worked properly, and I found a new message in my Inbox. It said 'R. Harrison, CEO' in the From field.

I texted Courtney: *He answered.*

She replied: *OMG. BRT.*

I stared at the screen for sixteen minutes, alone with my deafened senses, until Courtney burst through my bedroom door and landed on the bed next to me.

"You didn't open it yet?"

"I was waiting for you! You said you'd be right here, so I waited. You're late." I grinned at her.

"Oh my god, open it already." She couldn't move her eyes from the screen.

Neither could I.

I clicked the message and it popped open.

Ellen,

What a great surprise! Of course I remember you. You're still my favorite Yooper. I'd love to get together while you're in town. I'm a Credit Union CEO now—it's more fun than it sounds—and I live in the city. No more farm town for me! I even carry a briefcase to work every day. Go figure.

Let me know when you'll be in town and I'll make room for you on my schedule.

Take care, and thanks for emailing me!

Be cool.

Roy

"Oh my god," I whispered.

"He wants to see you." Courtney whispered back.

"I know. I can't believe this." I wondered if panic attacks usually start with a thundering heart beat. Or shortness of breath. I clicked reply, wondering what in the world I was going to write back.

"Don't answer him right away," said Courtney. "Or even today. He waited four days to answer you. You can't respond within ten minutes. That looks bad."

"You're right. Okay." My breath released in a gush,

and I felt my shoulders relax. "Yes. I'll take a day or two to figure out what I'm going to say."

"At least two days," said Courtney. "That's half the time he took to get back to you. Remember, you're being Elle. You're old. Well, older than thirteen. You don't get too excited about things anymore."

"Right. Got it." I closed the message.

We stared at each other.

Elle: April 13, 2008

Stella didn't bother saying hello when I called her. "Ellen. Good. This is good."

"What? Is everything okay?"

"Yes. Sorry." She swallowed. "I just found out Elyse—Mom—is speaking at an event at her park. On Thursday."

"This Thursday? Like, in three days?" My stomach fluttered. This was happening way too fast. It should take much longer than one Google search and three days to resurrect a deceased mother.

"Yep. Mick is willing to deal with the boys, so I can travel light." Her voice sounded determined.

"What's your plan? Will we listen to her speak, then leave? Or will we accost her on one of her manicured pathways?" Every idea I had sounded ridiculous.

"I don't know. I thought we could sit and listen to her, then decide."

"Okay, so if we decide we want to meet her, do we just walk up to her and introduce ourselves?"

"I don't know! I just—look. We can't not go, now that we know where she is. And I don't want to contact her ahead of time, in case we decide we don't want to meet her. This is like the Marines. Their preliminary maneuvers. What do they call it?" She paused. "Reconnaissance."

We were both silent for a couple of beats.

"Hmm. I'm guessing we'll want to talk to her, judging from her newspaper article and the pictures I found on the internet. She looks and sounds like someone we'd like. Hey," I said, "maybe I'll end up with a parent, after all. An apparent parent."

"That's the other reason I called. Fossil isn't doing so well. He has pneumonia. The young nurse—the one who looks twelve years old—said he's strong as an ox, and he'll pull through this. The older nurse, the one Fossil calls Nurse Crotcherson, said this might be his death sentence."

I remembered my last words to him and shuddered. Though he took up a microscopic space in my heart, I hoped my angry name-calling wouldn't be the last thing he heard me say. "Let's go with the ox prognosis. I'll muster up some positive thoughts."

"Either way, it's risky for me to leave right now.

But I feel like this is our chance to observe Mom without her knowing. And we'll get to hear her talk, see her move." She paused. "I sound like a stalker or something."

I laughed. "No, I get it. And you're right. This is our chance. Let's go."

We planned to leave in two days.

When I asked Mrs. Whitcomb if Althea could stay with her for a few days, she agreed before I finished speaking.

"Althea and I will have a grand time." Mrs. Whitcomb clasped her hands in front of her chest. "My land, it'll be like a slumber party!" She listed the activities she and Althea would enjoy: a rousing game of Aggravation, a few hands of Gin Rummy, maybe a cup of hot cocoa. "Maybe we can begin our knitting lessons!"

Al-chick would be in good hands.

March 13, 2001

The next day, I talked to Ruth.

I felt like I talked for hours—first about my mother, then about Fossil, and Boyd, and Roy, and Stella, and finally about you, my little seed pod, safe in my belly—and Ruth never interrupted once. We were sitting in the lobby, but it was a Wednesday and I'd just finished cleaning rooms, so it was quiet. When I was finished talking, I was thirsty and tired, and I slumped back on the chair with a sigh.

"Elle," said Ruth—she was the first one who ever called me Elle—"how old are you?"

Ruth had already hired me, but when she asked me about my age I figured she was looking for a way out. Why would she want me and my luggage? What did I expect her to do, harbor a pregnant, underaged runaway?

"Elle?"

"Sorry." I shook my head to clear my mind. It didn't work. "I'm...fifteen. I'll be sixteen next June."

Ruth looked at me, her back straight, ankles crossed, her perfect hands on her knees, skirt smooth. She could have been a picture in a magazine. I felt like a dried up mud puddle in contrast.

"Well, that might pose a problem," she said, subtly narrowing her eyes in thought. She took a breath, like she was going to say something, but she didn't. Then she took another breath and said, "let's review. You need a place to stay, and your truck towed to the junk yard. I can help you with those things. You also need to finish high school, and have a baby, and you have no photo ID because you're not yet old enough to drive. These last three items are going to give us a bit of grief, but I have some ideas that might help us."

Did you notice what she said, Al-bug? She said 'us'. When I heard her say that word, I thought I might burst. I had to pinch the inside of my arm and clear my throat before I could answer her without squeaking.

"What are your ideas?" I asked. I was sitting up straight now, full of energy again. Ruth brought me a glass of water and I drank it down in one motion while she thought about how to answer my question.

"Are you up for a little tour of The Phoenix Hotel?"

"I—I've already had the tour. I've seen every inch of this place, and cleaned most of it."

"Aah, but you haven't seen what I'm about to show you." She smiled, and again I thought of Mary Poppins, with her spoon full of sugar and her carpetbag full of goodies, and I knew I could trust Ruth.

"You make everything seem less...bleak." I told her. "I'll never know how to thank you for that."

"Oh, thank you! What a marvelous compliment." I followed her to the laundry room, taking the stairs the way we always did when we weren't pushing carts or carrying things. Ruth always said we should take every opportunity to exercise, and I'd already adopted this particular habit.

"I do like the laundry room, Ruth. It's nice and warm in the winter. But I still don't see—"

"Now don't be impatient." She smiled, and beckoned me beyond the double-line of washers and around the end of the dryers into a dark corner with a locked door marked Employees Only. I'd thought this door was to access the rear of the dryers for maintenance purposes. "That's one place this door leads," she said, "but, it also leads to the answer to your current dilemma." We walked down a short hall to another door, which she unlocked with the clutch of keys she always carried. She opened this second door with a flair, and gestured grandly for me to enter as she flicked on the lights.

The door was painted bright yellow and opened into a small room that looked like someone had taken an entire house and shrunk it down to fit into this tiny space. There was a single bed, a sink, a tiny refrigerator, a two-burner stove and four cupboards—two above the countertop, and two below. There was also a chair and a table, and a love seat pushed up against the wall.

Ruth leaned into the doorway just far enough for me to hear her. She wouldn't step into the room. "It's small, I know, but you can live here rent-free, at least until the next corporate meeting, in January. The owner, Mr. Hudson, stays here if we're booked solid."

"It's perfect." I smiled at Ruth and wondered how I was so lucky to walk into her hotel, of all the hotels in Chicago. "It's bigger than my truck, and it won't get towed away while I'm sleeping."

Gradually, Ruth revealed her entire plan for me: I would continue to work at The Phoenix as a maid and a front desk clerk, and I would pay for my room by working for two days without pay each week. She insisted on calling Fossil to verify my name and age, and to let him know I was okay. She also insisted on my writing to him every month, which I hated, because I didn't feel like he deserved to know about us, but I respected Ruth too much to tell her that.

I'm sure she knew, anyway.

Althea: April 13, 2008

Finally, my opportunity came a-knockin', as they say. I answered on the first knock.

"I have to go to Minneapolis," said Mom. She was slicing an onion and her face kept twisting in an effort to prevent her eyes from watering. "Stella's picking me up."

"What happened?"

"She found our mother, and she's speaking at her park on Thursday." Mom sniffed, but I couldn't tell whether it was the onion or her mother that was making her teary-eyed. "It's a park dedication, or welcome ceremony, or something."

"I can't wait to see the park! When are we leaving?"

"You're not." She stopped slicing and looked at me, knife in midair. "You can stay with Mrs. Whitcomb. I'll only be gone two nights, three at the most."

"Okay. I'll miss Aunt Stella." I tried to sound disappointed, like I was missing out on a trip to DisneyWorld. "And I'll miss my…grandma. Wow, that sounds crazy. If our family tree was a cabinet, it would be Old Mother Hubbard's Cupboard, until now. Now it's more like a survivalist's cupboard, stuffed so full the doors won't close." I scooped up the onion skins and tossed them into the sink. "Are you sure you won't need me?"

Mom smiled sadly. "Thanks, Al. You're so thoughtful. But this is something Stella and I need to do by ourselves, and I think the time together will be good for me and Stella. We need to decide what our next steps will be. Besides, you don't need to miss any more school this semester."

"What are you going to do there? Just attend the presentation?"

"We're going to go, yes. After that, I'm not so sure." She scraped the diced onions into the pan, where the garlic was just starting to sizzle. "I'll tell you all about it when I get back. I'm leaving tomorrow."

"Tomorrow! Wow, okay." I tried to look uncertain, as if I wasn't truly prepared for this opportunity, which I'll call luck, landing in my lap.

***

As soon as we finished eating dinner and doing dishes, I said I had homework to do and ran into my room. I never waited until Sunday night to do homework, but Mom didn't seem to notice. She was in her room, packing for Minneapolis.

I texted Courtney: *Mom leaving tomorrow. Gone 2-3*

nights.

Courtney answered immediately: *OMG. U going 2 Mad?*

I texted back: *Yep. Emailing him now.*

I opened my laptop and searched for trains to Madison. After ten minutes of searching, I had to accept the fact: there was no train from Chicago to Madison. I'd have to ride a bus. The thought of a bus ride, stuffy and swaying and filled with crying, snot-nosed children and old, unshaven men, made me gag. I'd only ever rode a city bus, and even a short ride had seemed way too long.

The bus left for Madison at 10:30 a.m. on Tuesday, and I'd have to get to Union Station to buy the ticket, then the Canal Street bus station to catch the bus. I'd need to take two trains to get to Union Station, but it looked like that would be the easy part.

My email to Roy was a bit rushed—I told him I could meet him somewhere near the University for coffee on Tuesday afternoon, and that my conference was shorter than I thought it would be.

I flipped open my phone and texted Courtney: *No train. Bus only.*

She replied: *OMG. What U going 2 do?*

I pressed buttons, wishing more than ever I had a smart phone. *Will miss 1 day school.*

Write a note from your Mom. Teachers won't care.

I could catch the early evening bus from Madison back to Chicago, returning at 9:10 p.m. I'd either have to sneak into Courtney's house for the night or tell Mrs. Whitcomb I was at Courtney's, but I wouldn't even get back to our neighborhood until at least 10 p.m. I'd never been out by myself that late at night. Maybe I was better off catching the early morning train from Madison, and just staying in the Madison bus station all night. I felt like a private eye, planning an all-night stake-out.

I texted Courtney again. I wished she was here, so I could stop wasting time punching the buttons on my stupid flip phone. *I might miss 1 nite too.*

Say ur staying @ my house.

K.

This plan was almost out of control, like a balloon about to pop.

The next morning, I presented a note in my best handwriting, signed with Mom's curlicue signature, to the school office so I would be excused from all of my classes on Tuesday. The secretary barely glanced at the note before stamping it so I could present it to my teachers. Other mothers emailed the school, and I was never so thankful to have a technologically stunted mother who still hand-wrote everything.

After school, I raced home to Mrs. Whitcomb's, eager to wipe down the kitchen and bathroom. I had so much energy, I could have sprinted to Madison without stopping. We spent the evening playing gin rummy, but I was so distracted I missed three plays and Mrs. Whitcomb won by a landslide.

Roy's email was waiting for me when I checked at bedtime. We were set to meet at the Steep 'N Brew at 4 p.m. I answered him quickly to confirm, then climbed into Mrs. Whitcomb's guest bed.

Everything was falling into place.

I spent the night going over my schedule in my mind, from train to train to bus ticket station, to bus stop, to Steep 'N Brew, and back again. By the time the sun rose again I was exhausted.

"Don't forget," I told Mrs. Whitcomb as I was on my way out the door, "I'm staying at Courtney's tonight."

"You are? Your mother didn't mention that."

"Oh, she must have forgotten." I struggled to maintain eye contact, and focused on her shiny glasses frame on the bridge of her nose instead. "Courtney and I are doing a project at school, so I'm just staying over so we can work on it." I swallowed hard and hoped my face wasn't as red as it felt. If Mrs. Whitcomb remembered Courtney and I weren't even in the same grade, I'd be busted before I went anywhere. I hoped she didn't look too closely at my backpack, which appeared soft and squishy instead of its usual boxy textbook shape.

"Okay, dear. Are you stopping here after school?"

"No, I'll just go straight to Courtney's after school. I'll see you tomorrow after school. Thanks, Mrs. Whitcomb!"

"Okay, bye now, dear." She had followed me to the door, and stood there now, waving at me down the hall. I didn't breathe until I had descended both sets of stairs and walked outside the building. There, I took a couple of deep breaths, then started running for the train station. I had to get to the Canal Street bus stop before 10:30.

Buying the ticket was smoother than I'd expected. I had all of my money with me, in case I needed cab fare or food in Madison, but I only had fifty bucks in the change purse I pulled out. The rest was hidden away in an inside zipper pocket. The ticket line was long, which probably worked in my favor. By the time I got to the window, the clerk must have been tired. She barely glanced at my face before taking my cash and printing out my ticket.

By the time I had my ticket and ran back outside, it was 9:57. If I waited for the red line El train, I might be late and miss the bus. I'd checked the distance on Google Maps, and it was just over two miles to the bus stop. I started running, dodging between people, sprinting across intersections, my backpack bouncing up and down on my hips. I let the excitement take over, and rushed almost past the bus stop. A small knot of people clustered outside the shelter, enjoying the sunshine. The bus pulled up right after I caught my breath.

I slipped in between a mother and toddler and a businessman in a suit and handed the bus driver my ticket on the way by.

"You got ID?"

"Me? Not with me."

"How old are you? You gotta be eighteen to ride by yo-self."

"I'm fifteen." I lifted my chin. I'd pass easily for fifteen, I figured, but probably not eighteen. "But I ride this bus all the time. I'm going to Madison, to visit my dad. I go every month."

We stared at each other for a minute while the people behind me started getting restless. Someone called out, "No wonder this bus always runs late!" Someone else yelled, "you never check ID for anyone else! Get on the road!"

The bus driver sighed and shook his head. "Go ahead. But I'm watching you."

I scuttled back to a seat about halfway back and settled in next to the window. I set my backpack on the seat next to me so no one would block me in. The bus was only about half full, but aside from the one businessman, the passengers were what I'd expected: crying kids and stubble-faced men. It smelled like stale vomit but looked clean, even the windows.

The bus rolled out, changing gears and whooshing out the air from the air brakes. The gentle sway soon lulled me, and I laid my head on my backpack and dozed off.

Elle: April 14, 2008

Stella's plan to drive through Chicago on her way to Minneapolis would have nearly tripled her drive time each way, so I flew to Minneapolis and met her at the hotel. We arrived in time for dinner, ate in the hotel restaurant, and settled into our room. Our hotel was situated near Elyse's park, but we weren't yet ready to see it. We walked through the neighborhood, carefully maintaining a minimum distance of two blocks from the park.

Back in the hotel room, we donned our pajamas and propped ourselves up on pillows, notebooks on our knees.

"They don't leave the guests notes here," I said. "Or fold the towels into animal shapes."

"Shabby, too shabby." Stella shook her head. "You could teach them a thing or two."

A minute ticked by.

"What do you remember about Mom?" My voice sounded small.

"Not much. I don't really have concrete memories. I have…vague impressions." She looked toward the far wall, then closed her eyes. "Graceful movement. Fun and laughter. Long, blonde hair. Musical voice. And certain colors—watery blues and greens." She opened her eyes and looked over at me. "What do you remember?"

I closed my eyes. "I remember art projects—drawing, painting. Fun and laughter." I nodded as I repeated Stella's words. "I remember eating soup."

"Tomato soup."

"Yes. And grilled cheese sandwiches. We put greasy fingerprints on our drawings." I paused, recalling a particular drawing of birds in a nest with grease-smudged eggs. "I remember winter. I think it was snowing outside. We were cozy and warm, wearing our smocks, painting on our little easels. Mom braided her hair and wrapped it into a bun. Our hair was tangled. I remember worrying about your hair, thinking you'd never get a comb through it. And we had dirty fingernails. After Heather came, I discovered the dark line near the tip of our fingernails didn't really belong there."

Stella breathed in, then paused. She did it again, then looked at me. "Did it seem like we took more baths after Mom left? Whenever I think of Heather, I think of water. We had toys for our bath after Heather came around."

I nodded. "I think you're right—we took a bath every day after Mom left. Heather used conditioner on our hair, and sprayed it with No More Tangles after washing it." We heard muffled thumps and bumps from the room next door. "And we stopped eating sugar and butter sandwiches."

Stella laughed. "I'd forgotten about those. Who feeds their children sugar and butter sandwiches?"

"I know! So gross. On white bread, too. A serious nutritional deficit."

"Was Mom a bad mom?"

I thought for a moment. "I hate to think so, but I'm not sure. I think she loved us, and kept us safe." I shrugged. "I have a whole photo album of proof that she did art projects and took lots of pictures of us."

"Did she have any friends at all? Anyone we can ask? I called Mrs. Heinonnen, but she was pretty tight-lipped."

"I don't remember anyone else ever visiting or hanging out." I sighed. "I'm a little scared, Stella."

Stella waited for me to continue.

"What if Mom isn't anything like our memories, and we're about to destroy all positive associations?" I folded my arms for warmth. "I'm not sure I can withstand losing my childhood again."

"We have to wait and see. And trust that all will go well." Stella sounded more confident than I felt.

We turned out the lights and settled in our beds, but neither of us slept more than a few scattered minutes.

***

Mom's park featured a small fountain and several statues of children's storybook characters. There were enough winding paths between the trees and bushes to play a rousing game of hide and seek, and we found two benches near the entrance labeled Ellen's Bench and Stella's Bench. Each bench had the phrase *Sweet memories are made here* carved in the back of it.

The center of the park reminded me of a tiny town square. A gazebo squatted near one end, and there were a few curvy rows of folding chairs bedecked with fabric bows. The two speakers and microphone stand were the only things that appeared out of place.

It was a beautiful setting for a wedding, a picnic, or a game of tag.

We selected two chairs about halfway back, on the left edge of the row. "In case we need to run," said Stella.

"You've never run." I grinned and bumped her shoulder with mine. "That was me. Remember?"

"You can sit on the edge, then. In case you run

again." She laughed.

Everyone was still settling into their seats when Elyse approached the microphone. She sounded extremely far away, as if I wore earplugs. The sun suddenly crested the hedges and my right eye watered. I'd stopped breathing when she uttered her first word, and Stella gripped my hand so hard I had no feeling in my fingers.

"Welcome to Harmony Park. I'm honored so many of you took time out of your day to come and enjoy my labor of love." Elyse gazed out over the audience. She seemed at home on the stage, as if she routinely spoke to crowds. She had no cards or notes—she simply spoke, each word straight from her heart.

"The creation and design of this park," she swept one arm out, "was inspired by my dear daughters. They were two of the purest souls you could ever hope to meet." She smiled at the crowd.

Stella and I shot mute questions at each other with our eyes.

"They loved art and nature, and I tried to combine those two passions here for everyone to enjoy. Please, be our guest at Harmony Park as often as you wish.

"I have established Harmony Foundation to maintain the park. All donations to Harmony Foundation will be used toward the care and maintenance of Harmony Park."

I saw stars. My chair felt like it had tilted, and I slid forward. Stella caught me.

She looked as rough as I felt. I closed my eyes and took a long, calm breath. I focused on a pointy piece of tree bark fifteen feet away. When I felt the anxiety subside, I turned to Stella.

"What do we do?" I whispered.

"I don't know." Stella dropped her head down. "The first moment I saw her, I thought I wanted to talk to her. But now," she looked back at Elyse, "I'm not so sure." Stella's face was as pale and translucent and delicate as Limoges china.

"If we wait, when will we have this chance again?"

"I know! Let's just sit here for a moment and collect ourselves," she said. "Let's take five more minutes before we make a decision."

I realized we were holding hands again, and I felt like a protective older sister looking out for four-year-old Stellie.

When the phone rang, all I felt was relief when I saw Althea's name on the Caller ID. The decision could be postponed.

Althea: April 14, 2008

I woke up to a singsong chant. The bus swayed gently, highlighting my vague nausea, and the air still smelled like stale body odor and ancient vomit. The rhythmic chant sounded like Maddy's son, Maddy's son. Someone kept shushing the chanter, but the chanter chanted on.

The chanter sounded far away, but the shusher sounded like she was right behind me. I suddenly realized what the chanter was saying: He wasn't saying Maddy's son; he was saying Madison. We must be close! I sat up and peered out the window, and sure enough, we were in a town. There weren't any skyscrapers, but I was pretty sure Madison was kind of a low-key, laid-back city. Not an in-your-face city.

Not many people walked the streets, but there were lots of bicyclists out this morning, all sailing smoothly past the bus in the narrow bike lane painted along the edge of the street. I wondered if Roy ever rode his bike to his CEO job, with his suit jacket and tie flapping in the breeze. Probably not.

I checked my phone—it was 1:00 p.m. The bus must have had a slight delay on the route, which gave me less time than I'd planned before I had to meet Roy. If I were in school right now, I'd be in Mrs. Warczinski's class, probably sitting there with my hand up waiting for her to call on me, which she wouldn't do because she believed in "giving everyone a chance to answer". As if the kids who didn't raise their hands really wanted to answer. I only wanted to answer her questions so we could move on to the next thing—time dragged in Mrs. Warczinski's class because we had to analyze everything so deeply. Why was the door in the story painted red? Maybe the author liked that color best, or maybe he gazed around his room and his eyes fell on something red before he noticed anything else. But no, Mrs. Warczinski had to infuse every word, every phrase with meaning and subtext and symbolism, and every story we read was ruined beyond enjoyment.

The bus pulled up to the bus stop and everyone stood, ready to file out the door. I whisked past the driver before he remembered to say anything to me and burst out to a cool, sunny day. I wasn't sure which direction to go—I'd memorized the Google map image, and had a copy in my bag, but I couldn't see a street sign from here and I didn't want to stand around near the bus stop figuring out which direction was which. I followed the bulk of the crowd, and paused once I rounded the corner to check the map. My stomach rumbled, reminding me I hadn't eaten for hours. I headed toward State Street in search of cheap food.

After eating an expensive turkey sandwich and downing a large bottle of water, I explored the Capitol building and walked around the streets. The clock seemed to crawl as I waited for 4:00 to roll around; I explored the entire neighborhood and part of the University grounds, and I even walked past Roy's credit union three times. I almost went in, but I didn't want him to see me in there and then recognize me again in the Steep 'N Brew.

I entered the coffee shop at half past three and stationed myself near the back wall where I could see everyone entering. I ordered a large caramel macchiato and pulled out my laptop. Malcolm had told me many writers hang out in coffee shops and write great American novels; I thought maybe I'd get started on mine, about a girl in search of her dad. Plus, the laptop gave me something to hide behind if I changed my mind about meeting Roy. Malcolm had also told me it's always smart to have a back-up plan, but he wasn't really talking about a situation like this.

At ten minutes to four, a balding man in a suit walked through the door and glanced around the room. He stood in line to order a drink, and another balding man walked up behind him. The second one looked more alert, like he was especially interested in every customer in the whole place. I didn't have a printed photo of Roy, so I opened the file on my laptop to compare the faces to the image in the Habitat article. It's amazing how similar bald or balding men look, I thought. They both had light brown hair—maybe like dark sand—and they had similar jawlines, at least from my vantage point, which was a good thirty feet away. They both wore suits—one gray, one blue. I desperately needed Courtney's eye for detail right this minute.

The line moved quickly, and the second Roy candidate was ordering his drink. He looked around again after paying for his coffee, and I waved without meaning to. Kind of like raising my hand for Mrs. Warczinski—it just happened. I felt my face smiling, but I didn't mean to do that, either. He was walking toward me slowly, his sandy eyebrows raised.

"Were you waving at me?"

"Um, yes. Are you Roy? Roy Harrison?"

He looked around the room again before answering, as if he wanted to make sure there weren't any others who would answer to this name. "Yes, I am. Can I help you?"

"I'm Ellen's daughter."

"You're—" He cleared his throat and tried again. "Ellen Marchand's daughter?"

"Yes." This might sound shameful, but I enjoyed his slight discomfort. He wasn't sure how to handle this. Wait until I tell you the rest of the story, I thought. You're really going to freak. "You can sit down, if you'd like."

He looked down at his hand, already pulling a chair back, and shrugged one shoulder as if to say I might as well as he sank onto the seat. "Thanks. Where's Ellen?"

"She couldn't make it." We stared at each other.

"Here you go, hon." The barista had walked his coffee out to the table, probably wondering why he hadn't lingered near the delivery counter to get it himself. She set it down with a soft thump, her tattoo peeking out from her sleeve. I caught the word 'believe' before it disappeared again. "I thought you left the building! Then I saw you hiding over here in the corner."

"Thank you," Roy said, and we resumed our staring. I would forever associate the scent of fresh coffee with my dad's face. My real dad's real face.

"My name," I paused with what I hoped was dramatic tension, like I saw on TV, "is Althea."

When Roy continued to stare, I added, "Jerry Garcia named me."

"You—" He cleared his throat again. "You look like my little sister. When she was your age. Wait, how old are you?"

"I'm probably exactly as old as you think I am." I was getting into this dramatic tension thing, enjoying the slow delivery of information and carefully placed pauses. "I just turned thirteen."

"To be clear." Now Roy was pulling his own dramatic tension tricks. "Are you saying you're my…relative?"

"Yes." I watched his face, waiting for a reaction to my next declaration. "I'm your daughter."

He ran his hand through his hair, or at least he tried to, but he must have forgotten his hair had left his head long ago.

"Are you sure? I'm not saying I don't believe you, but —how do you know? And why didn't Ellen tell me?"

"I don't have DNA proof or anything, but I'm sure."

"And Ellen told you about meeting me? Back in 1995?"

"Not exactly. Look, here are the facts." I numbered them on my fingers to illustrate my evidence. "For one, I know my mom only had one wild weekend of her whole entire life, and that was the weekend of the Grateful Dead concert in Chicago. For two, she named me based on the song Althea because Jerry Garcia sang it right to her. For three, I was born nine months after that concert. And four, I found your name written on a torn piece of paper in an envelope with her concert ticket." Oops. I hadn't meant to name this last fact, but it tumbled out before I could control it.

"Wow. I can't believe I didn't know about this." Roy looked stunned and unsure, like a little kid who lost his mom in the store.

"And five, which I just discovered today, we have the same eye color. Mom has blue eyes, like everyone else in her family, but mine are hazel. Just like yours."

"So Ellen has been a single mother all these years?"

"Yep." Why was this so hard to understand?

"I didn't mean for that to happen." He shook his head. He licked his lips and looked at the table. "I can't believe she never called me."

"Well, the paper I found only had a partial phone number on it, if that helps."

"But she could have found me. You found me." He looked up at me now, searching my face with his eyes.

"I'm not sure she was looking for you."

"Have you had—Are you—"

I waited for him to figure out what he wanted to say. I hadn't thought about how this would affect Roy—this was the first time he was hearing the news of my existence! I'd known I had a dad out in the world someplace for the past thirteen years, but Roy had no idea he had a daughter. I guess he was handling it pretty well, considering he was expecting to reunite with a fun teenager from the UP and he ended up getting a dour-looking teenager from north Chicago who claimed to be directly descended from him.

"I just want to know, is your life good? Are you happy? Is Ellen happy? Do you need anything?" Apparently his vocabulary deserted him in times of stress. I saw this happen on TV once, when someone was rendered speechless as a fish whenever something caused them anxiety.

"We're okay. Happy." I considered his question—he clearly wanted to know if we needed him all those years, or if we were succeeding on our own. "We are a tribe of two. We do everything together."

Roy's face grew more serious, if that was possible, and his eyes narrowed. "Wait a minute, does Ellen know you're here?"

Oops again. Why hadn't I seen that question coming? And how was I going to answer it? My unfaithful stomach dropped into my shoes. And I had to pee.

"Not really, no. She's in Minneapolis right now."

"You can't just travel around by yourself. Where do you live?"

"Chicago. But don't worry, I'm catching the bus tonight and I'll be back home by morning."

"The bus!" He looked horrified. "Oh, I don't think so. You can't ride the bus by yourself. You're only thirteen." Now he sounded like a dad, and part of me liked the concern I heard in his voice. The other part of me didn't like having to answer to someone I'd just met. Then I remembered it was all my doing, this meeting. Damn Courtney's cyber skills, I thought, and this nearly made me giggle.

I breathed deep and clenched my fists beneath the table to kill the giggle.

"I already have my ticket." I waved my hand to show it was no big thing, riding the bus. "Don't worry, I'm from Chicago. I know how to handle myself." This last came out a bit on the surly side, and I hoped I didn't insult him.

"That may be, but we need to call your mother and let her know where you are and that you're alright." His tone held no room for negotiation, but I tried anyway.

"I don't need to call her," I said. "She's busy with her sister and her mom. Kind of. Whatevs." Now *my* vocabulary was failing. Malcolm would be appalled. I took a deep breath, hearing Roberta tell me to center myself. I felt anything but centered.

"If you're here, telling me that you're my daughter, I'm going to act like your dad." He caught himself. "I *am* your dad. Wow. I still can't believe it. I have two sons, and if one of them took a bus to Chicago, you can bet I'd want to know about it." He took a sip of his coffee, grimacing at the lukewarm temperature. "Bad things can happen."

I tried changing the subject. Calling Mom was the absolute last thing I wanted to do—she would flip! No way could I let her find out I had left the neighborhood, lied to Mrs. Whitcomb, forged her signature on a note at school. I'd even crossed the state line. The list of crimes I'd committed would destroy Mom and she would never trust me again. I had to make him forget about calling her, fast.

"I just wanted to meet you, to find out where I came from. That's all."

He started to speak, probably to tell me we had to call Mom, but I interrupted and kept talking until he gave up. I knew this wasn't a solid plan, but it was the only one I had. "I wanted to find out about you, what you like, where you work, what your life is like. I wanted to see if I look like you, because I look a little bit like Mom, but it's not like I'm a clone or anything, and I wanted to see who shared her one wild weekend back in 1995, and who saw Jerry Garcia sing my name. Have you ever watched the YouTube video of him singing Althea? It's bad. The song looks so much better on paper than it sounds at the concert. I hope it sounded better in person—I can't believe Mom liked the name, after hearing the way he sang it on stage." I babbled on, but I could tell by his expression he wasn't going to give up the idea of calling Mom. He was like a cat waiting for the mouse to stick its nose out of the hole. Patient and watchful and ready to pounce.

"What's her number?" He said as soon as I stopped to take a breath.

"I can't tell you. I'll be in so much trouble, I don't even know what she'll do. She'll probably ground me or take away my laptop or make me apologize to Mrs. Whitcomb. Definitely apologize to Mrs. Whitcomb."

"Who's Mrs. Whitcomb?"

"Our neighbor. I'm staying with her. She thinks I'm staying at my friend Courtney's tonight." I looked down at the table as I spoke. I focused on a crumb the barista had missed when she last wiped the table. "I'm a good kid, honest." I forced my eyes to meet his. "I never do anything like this."

"Why don't I call her," he said, speaking slowly like he was trying to coax a rabbit out of a hole, "and tell her everything is okay and you shouldn't be punished. You're just curious, and you're safe, and I can drive you home."

I didn't know if I wanted to ride with Roy. He wasn't a stranger, exactly, but then again, I didn't really know him. Just because he donated some spare DNA back in 1995 didn't mean he wasn't some kind of freaky pervert or something. I studied his face. He didn't look perverted. He looked like someone's dad, like a concerned parent. Kind of like I pictured my dad to look, but with less hair than my imagination had endowed him.

"Look. I just wanted to meet you, okay? I wanted to know what you look like, what you've been doing all these years...Mom never mentions you." He flinched at this, but it was a surface flinch. He must have thought we sat around pining for him all the time, while he went on with his life, oblivious of the biological deposit he'd made during Mom's one wild weekend. "I didn't mean for anything…major…to happen. I just wanted to make sure you're real."

"Nothing major? What did you think, I would just say 'oh, hi, yes, I'm Roy, the one who met your mom in 1995. Okay then, well, have a good life.' That's not how it works." He threw up his hands and I could see frustration on his face. His expression twisted into disbelief and maybe even hurt feelings. How could I hurt his feelings, when he hadn't even known I was alive until ten minutes ago?

"I didn't think it all the way through. I thought I did, but apparently I didn't." A weak defense, but I couldn't think of anything else on the fly.

"We need to call your mom."

"You're like a parrot! Please keep my mom out of this. I'll get myself home and if there's any trouble, I'll take the consequences."

He narrowed his eyes a little and spoke in a gentle tone. "Have you ever done anything like this before?"

"No. *Obvi*. That's why I'm not very good at it." If I was talking to Mom right now, we would have cracked up. I looked at Roy from the corner of my eye and I didn't detect one tiny bit of laughter on his face. He looked scared and confused and doubtful.

"Call your mom. Non-negotiable. I'll deliver you safely, and I'll even talk to Mrs. Whitcomb. If one of my boys was in this situation, their safety would be far more important than whether or not they had lied or run away or anything else."

I rolled my eyes. Roy was 28% parental, 56% stern

and concerned, and 16% frustrated. Overall, not too friendly.

I fidgeted and rearranged my feet below the table. I sighed. The biggest sigh of my whole life. I knew I was beat; I had no recourse. My hands shook a little as I pulled out my phone and punched in Mom's number. The coffee shop went on around us but the level of the background noise somehow escalated to a grating volume while my voice shrank so much I feared Mom wouldn't recognize it.

Her voice sounded breathless and close when she answered. "Hey, Al-chick! What's up?"

"Hi, Mom?" I cleared my throat and watched Roy watching me. "I have something to tell you."

March 15, 2001

I called our micro-apartment The Sunshine Room, a name inspired by the bright yellow door. Ruth's claustrophobia wouldn't allow her to enter the tiny, tight space, but I found it comforting. The Sunshine Room felt like a safe haven, tucked away below the city. A secret vault. I painted the walls sky blue and hand-lettered my favorite Arthur Ashe quote above the miniature sink and stove: "Start where you are. Use what you have. Do what you can."

We lived there until February, because the corporate meeting Ruth had mentioned was rescheduled due to the owner's wife's unplanned surgery. Those few months spent snuggled beneath The Phoenix gave me time to think about my childhood and how I was raised, and how I wanted to raise you. I never want to let you down, Althea, and I know I will sometimes, but I hope you realize when it happens that I didn't intend to disappoint you. And I can promise you this: I will never, ever leave you.

Months later, after we'd moved in with Ruth and you emerged, I thought perhaps I'd been depressed before we lived in the Sunshine Room, and my meager nesting efforts helped pull me out of it.

Letters were mailed to Fossil every month. I mailed them on the first so I could enjoy the rest of the month, like taking a pill as soon as you wake up so you can enjoy the rest of the day.

The first few letters were returned to me at The Phoenix, so I stopped putting a return address on them. There's nothing more depressing than writing a letter to a father who lied to you your whole life, and then seeing it come back in the mail unopened. It was like a slap in the face all the way from the UP. Cold and stunning.

I can still feel the overwhelming rejection I felt when I saw those letters come back. It takes my breath away. Who rejects their own child? Only a monster.

I also wrote letters to Stella, which I mailed to Ariel, and Stella wrote back to me, keeping Ariel busy running back and forth to the post office. It sounded like Stella and Fossil were getting along better than when I was there. Maybe it was a good thing I'd left. Stella went a little wild for a couple of years, but I suppose she'd learned that by watching me.

I missed my sister. I still miss her now, even though we talk on the phone every week or so, but it's never been the same. She was my shadow, and when you're someone's shadow and that someone moves away, you're no longer a shadow. You're left exposed, alone, defenseless.

Ruth arranged for me to take the GED exams, so I wouldn't have to return to high school. I found some study guides online, and took the exams all at once during a day-long GED marathon. I passed everything on my first try. And that's how I finished school before Stella did. I'm not proud of dropping out of high school, but having the GED certificate helps me feel like I still made it through.

Ruth also helped me get a photo ID. She called Fossil, and his secretary Nancy, and the woman at the County Courthouse back in Houghton County, and the Judge, and she must have known a magical incantation, because she persuaded all of those people that I needed to be legally emancipated so I could be legally responsible for myself and my actions. Fossil was the only one who didn't balk at the idea.

We worked together like we were mother and daughter—I anticipated what she needed me to do, and did it without being told. I left the guests little welcoming notes in the bathroom, to make the guests feel like they were visiting friends. Many of them called the front desk and left a message to thank me for the lovely note; some of them wrote back, and I'd find notes when I cleaned the rooms.

She's never admitted it, but I'm sure Ruth spoke to Mr. Hudson, and she may have persuaded him to promote me.

Ruth was my cheerleader and my mentor.

And so the fairy tale ends. Or does it? The king shirked his duties, the queen disappeared, the princesses grew up. But you're the princess now, and your responsibility is to yourself and your future.

Accept help when you need it, make wise decisions, and don't be afraid to follow your dreams even if it means leaving

everything you know behind.
I will never leave you.

Love,
Mom

Elle: April 14, 2008

By the time I flipped my phone shut, Stella had signed the guest book, grabbed two Harmony Park brochures, and returned to my side.

"Where are we headed?" She asked.

"Althea's in Madison." I stared at Stella. "With Roy."

"Roy?" She stared back at me. "As in Farm Town? What in the world?"

"I have no idea. I don't know how she found him, or how she even knew who to look for." I took a deep breath and looked around for Elyse. I didn't see her at first, but then I noticed her bent over an elderly lady in a wheelchair. They looked like old friends. I wondered if the wheelchair woman knew about Elyse's daughters. "I guess we wait to meet Mom?"

"Of course!" Stella started walking down the path

to exit the park. "We're not dilly dallying here now. We're in the middle of a rescue!" She sounded like Christopher Robin, setting out to find Winnie-the-Pooh.

"I'm lucky Roy's a nice guy. Or at least, he sounds nice, and he's responsible enough to make her call me instead of letting her get herself back to Chicago or—worse—" I stopped, unable to voice the imagined trauma Althea could have endured. *Hopefully she would have endured and lived to tell about it,* I silently corrected myself. "Stella."

She grabbed my arm and dragged me forward. "No breakdowns now. We'll have time for that later. We can have multiple breakdowns, one for the generation before us, one for the generation after us. But we can't do it now."

We ran through the hotel lobby to our room, repacked our bags, dropped off the key and fled the hotel. Stella's GPS informed us we'd be on the road for over four hours, but we made it in three and a quarter.

"You got us here ahead of schedule," I said as I watched the street signs, ready to direct her next turn.

"I have a V8. And a GPS. You really should embrace technology." Stella grinned. "I feel so much better, being in the same city with your girl."

"Thank you so much. You didn't even hesitate, and I can't tell you—" I felt tears welling.

"Don't. We've had an emotional week. I'm here for you, same as always, same as you are for me." Stella squeezed my forearm. "We don't need to examine these things—they just are."

"Turn here! Turn right!"

"Okay, okay, settle down. Be calm, now. Don't screw up the directions. What's the next street we need?"

"Panfish Court. What kind of name is that, anyway?" I flicked a tear off my cheek.

"It's a magical name, where the damsel Althea awaits rescue." She glanced at me.

"You're good. I can't think of anyone else I'd want with me when I'm in the clinch."

Stella laughed. "In the clinch! Oh, here it is."

"And here's the house: number 10110. How binary."

Althea was running out the door, barreling toward the truck. I jumped out and clutched her to me, clenching my eyes and hanging on as if she might slip away if I relaxed my grip. Eventually I noticed a figure standing a few feet behind her, waiting patiently for our reunion to disband. Stella hopped out of the truck and ran around to us, tapping Althea on her shoulder and taking over my manic hug so I could talk to Roy.

I cleared my throat, hoping my voice wouldn't fail me. "Roy." I shook his hand. "Thank you so much. I'm so sorry about this, she's never done anything like this before."

He started speaking before I'd finished. "Ellen, I

hope I did the right thing. I just wanted to make sure she got home in one piece. Don't be too hard on her."

We both laughed nervously, then we both glanced at his house, where his wife's face peered at us through the glass. "My sons are in bed, but Lisa—would you like to meet Lisa? She's had a crazy day." He shook his head, then turned toward the house and called in through the door. "Honey? Come on out and meet everyone." He walked back to me, hands in his pockets. "She didn't want to intrude, but we all might as well meet each other."

Stella and Althea parted, but Stella kept her arm around Al. I went to Al's other side and put my arm around her, too.

"Here she is," said Roy. "Lisa, this is Ellen, Althea's mother, and Stella, Ellen's sister."

"Today my most important title is Althea's aunt," said Stella. She removed her right hand from Althea long enough to shake Lisa's hand. I shook Lisa's hand too, and we both murmured something about how nice it was to meet each other.

"This is so surreal," said Roy. "I still can't believe this happened. And it's been happening for thirteen years!" He looked at each of us in turn, his gaze finally settling on my face. "Why didn't you call me, Ellen? I feel like I abandoned you, but I didn't even know what you were going through."

"I thought about calling you. I did. But I was

dealing with my dad, and then I had to find a place to live, and—I don't know—I was fifteen." I looked at their house, their landscaped yard, their shoes. There was no help to be found. "I guess that's my only excuse. Apparently I could only deal with one problem and one solution at a time. Once I found a place to live, I knew I could make it on my own."

"And why didn't you ever get married?" Roy looked so sad, I wanted to comfort him. "Or at least find someone to help you?"

I squeezed Roy's arm. "I was raising a daughter, managing a luxury hotel, and proving to my dad, not that he was watching, that I could do it all. I completely forgot to get married."

He smiled and shook his head.

"I told him about the torn phone number," said Althea. When I raised on eyebrow in question, she added,"the one in your envelope."

"*That's* how you started out on this goose chase? By snooping in my closet?"

"Yep. A name, a partial phone number, a Grateful Dead concert ticket…voila!" She looked proud of her cyber-sleuthing talent.

"Don't pat yourself on the back too quickly," I said. "You are in trouble. Big trouble." I started counting on my fingers. "Snooping, lying to Mrs. Whitcomb, crossing State lines, associating with an unknown—" I gestured toward Roy, "—but, lucky for us, responsible adult, and I'm sure I can come up with a few more infractions on the ride home. You might be grounded so long, I won't have to worry about becoming a grandmother until I'm actually old enough to be one."

Lisa shuffled her feet back and forth a little, then excused herself and went back into the house.

"I'm going to let you guys settle this. I'd invite you in, but the boys are sleeping—or trying to—and everyone has had such a crazy day, and it's late, and—"

"No, no, Roy, we don't need to come in. We're only a couple of hours from home. We'll keep moving, and deal with Al-chick on the way."

"Ellen," he said, handing me a card. "Keep in touch, okay? I want to help. I want to get to know her. She's a remarkable girl." He gave her a half-hug, then squeezed her arm. He turned toward me and touched my shoulder. "Don't be too hard on her, okay? She was just curious. And everything turned out okay."

I nodded and shook his hand, then joined Stella and Althea in the truck. Stella already had her GPS programmed to deliver us to my address.

The last thing I saw was Roy's silhouette, standing outside his brightly lit house, waving as we drove away. He looked solid and strong and sure.

As we left the neighborhood, Althea started defending herself. "I'm sorry I went against every rule in the world, but I have a right to know who my dad is." We sat in silence for a few seconds, so she started again.

"You never told me the whole story! And our family is crazy. Everyone leaves everyone else, and some people go back, but then they leave again, and some are dead, but they're really not." She swallowed and shifted in her seat. "I had to make sure, for myself, that Roy is normal, and regular, and alive, and I thought he kind of knew about me. I thought he knew you were pregnant at least. Like I said, completely in the dark. Living with the bats and mushrooms here. 'Cause you never tell me the. Whole. Story."

"I'm sorry too, Al. You're right, you're old enough now to hear the whole story. And I promise you will, soon." She sighed loudly, but I continued as if I hadn't heard her. "Look, let's wait until tomorrow to discuss this. Stella and I are exhausted and right now, I'm just happy you're alive and unharmed. I'm going to call Mrs. Whitcomb to let her know you're okay. She thinks this whole thing is her fault, because she believed you were staying at Courtney's! Who, by the way, is also in trouble with her mother right now."

"What's she in trouble for? She didn't even do anything!"

"She was your accomplice."

"Accomplice? Really? We didn't commit murder."

"No, but you fooled the world's nicest grandma lady, you directly disobeyed me, you snooped—". I stopped talking when she started mimicking me, saying everything I said a half-syllable after I said it.

"Althea," said Stella, "I don't want to butt in, but it's in your best interest to stop now, and await your punishment tomorrow. It's only going to get worse if you continue with this course of action."

"You know, you could have been a lawyer or a social worker or a crisis intervention manager." I said.

"Thank you. I'm actually all three, I just don't have the education or the titles to prove it," said Stella.

We chuckled and Althea slumped down in the back seat, hands crossed tightly across her chest. I stared at the road ahead, thanking the stars and the Universe and fickle old Fate for keeping her safe.

I'd never been so tired in all of my life.

When Stella parked in front of our building, I saw a shadow drifting back and forth in front of the lobby window. The door opened, and Mrs. Whitcomb stepped carefully outside.

"Oh my land, is she okay?" Mrs. Whitcomb sounded shaken. She held her hands out, then clutched them together again.

"Althea, you'd better apologize. She's been up worrying for hours." I glared at Althea, who ducked her head and spilled out of the truck in slow motion.

"I'm okay, Mrs. Whitcomb," Althea said quietly. She gave Mrs. Whitcomb a hug.

"Child, you scared me." Mrs. Whitcomb held Althea by the shoulders so she could look her in the face. "When your mom called, I had no idea you weren't right where you told me you'd be, at Courtney's place."

"I know." Althea looked up the street, then down at the ground. "I'm sorry. I hope you didn't worry too much."

"Any worrying is too much worrying, but don't you worry about me." Mrs. Whitcomb smiled. "It's all over, now that I can see you standing here, healthy and alive."

Stella and I climbed out of the truck and grabbed our bags from the back.

"I'm sorry, Mrs. Whitcomb," I said as I approached her. "I didn't realize I was leaving an escape artist with you. Last I checked, she was a homebody." I hugged the elderly woman and whispered "thank you" in her ear.

"No need to thank me, Elle." Mrs. Whitcomb shook her head. "And no need to apologize. I should've seen this one coming. This wasn't my first circus." She shrugged. "I probably should have insisted she stay and learn how to knit!"

Stella greeted Mrs. Whitcomb and we all headed inside.

❊❊❊

Stella left early the next morning, before Althea woke up. I rummaged in my closet until I found the answers to Althea's questions, the whole story to which she was entitled. The letter I'd written when she was a little girl.

"Good morning, Al-chicky." I said when she emerged from her room mid-morning. "I have something for you." I held out the fat envelope.

"What is it?"

"It's the whole story. I wrote this when you were little, so I wouldn't forget any details. Several times I wanted to give it to you, but there was never a good time, so…well, I'm doing it now."

She held the envelope in both hands as if it were holy scripture. "Thank you."

"Take your time, I'll be here when you're finished reading it."

An hour later, she found me in the living room. "Thanks, Mom," she said into my shoulder. She hugged me hard. "I'm sorry I made you worry. I will never do anything like that again."

I looked at her. "I know you won't. And like Roy —your dad—said, you were just curious, and everything turned out okay. So I've decided," I paused dramatically, "to ground you—for two weeks."

"I'll take it." She grinned. "I know I deserve more punishment than that, but I'm very sorry, and I'll make it up to you, and you're right, everything turned out okay." She sat still for a minute. "You know, I was careful. I knew what he looked like from pictures I found on the Internet, and I met him in a public place, and since he was expecting to meet you, I had time to check him out before he knew who I was."

"I've gotta hand it to you," I said, "you've got more moxie and more street smarts than I had at your age. Many times over the years I've thought about how lucky we both are that nothing happened to us back in those early days. We'll never know how lucky."

"We were born under lucky stars, that's what Courtney says. Some people are born under lucky stars, and some aren't, and by the time they're like your age, you can tell which are which."

We laughed, and relaxed a tiny bit, ready to make our way back to who we were before, even as we knew that was impossible. Lucky stars or not.

April 23, 2008

Towns grieve. They grieve for the young and for the old, and for everyone in between, when they pass from this life to the next.

The woman arrived in Iron Falls the morning of the funeral, having driven through the night.

She entered the funeral home five minutes before the funeral began, and squeezed into the back left corner as if she belonged there.

Elle: April 23, 2008

Althea looked like an adult in her black dress. She'd had to wear the one I'd given her for her birthday, since it was the only black dress she owned. I hoped she wouldn't forever associate that dress with death and sorrow.

"Coffee's on," said Stella.

I entered the kitchen with Althea on my heels, as she'd been since the moment three days ago when we heard that Fossil had passed away during the night. The morning nurse had entered his room on the day they'd planned to finally release him to go home, but he'd already left.

"Thanks." I put an arm lightly around Stella's shoulder as I poured myself a cup of coffee. "Do you need me to do anything?"

Stella leaned against the counter. We wore matching

dresses, which we'd purchased separately online without conferring with each other.

"No. I don't think there's anything to do." She watched her husband cross the room to the coffee pot. "Good morning, honey."

He bent down and kissed her cheek. "Good morning. How are you holding up?"

"I'm okay."

Mick greeted me and Althea, then took his cup into the living room to watch the news and talk to the boys. They were dressed in matching black dress pants and white button-down shirts, hair combed flat and pockets stuffed with mints. Someone at school had told them to eat a mint to avoid crying at a funeral, and they were determined to avoid crying at any cost. Especially in public.

"Until they start crying," Stella had told me. "Once they start, it's all over. They let it all out."

"As they should," I'd said.

I could hear Mick answering the boys' questions about the funeral. He repeated his advice on how to act and what to say to people. "'Thank you for coming' is a good one," he said. "And, 'it's good to see you.' Try to keep your hands out of your pockets. Just clasp them like this." He paused. "Let's see. No running, no pushing, no crawling. No squeezing between people. Wait your turn."

Mick appeared in the archway between the kitchen

and living room.

"The debriefing is complete," he said. "One more cup of coffee and we'll head over there."

***

The funeral, per Fossil's wishes, stated in the will we'd found in the files at his house, was arranged and hosted by Davenport's Funeral Home. It was a fifteen-minute drive from town. Fossil had requested cremation, so there wouldn't be a graveside service.

We'd arrived the day after he died, once again witnessing the parade of casserole-bearing townspeople. Brief, intense clutches from people I barely recognized, encouraging words from some I'd never met, offers of help from every single one of them. If you live in a small town and you're lonely, I thought, it's your own fault.

Stella, Althea and I had sifted through Fossil's papers and, finding everything organized, we started cleaning the house and determining which items to keep and which to sell or give away. By the time the day of the funeral arrived, we were nearly ready for a garage sale. We'd wait at least a month before listing the house with a real estate agent.

Many of the casserole-bearers were among the first group to arrive at the funeral home. We stood in a crooked receiving line in the foyer as everyone filed in. They paused at the photo collage we'd created at Fossil's kitchen table, murmuring memories and shuffling forward in search of weak coffee and sugar cookies.

It wasn't until after the funeral—after the tearful speeches, the shared memories and the eulogy Mick delivered—I noticed a tall, thin woman near the back of the room. She looked furtive, excusing herself to each person in turn as she worked her way out of the room, head down, dark glasses on.

I elbowed Stella and nodded toward the woman. "Is that?"

"Oh my god," said Stella. "Yes."

We moved together toward the woman. She'd just reached the door and was stepping into the hallway when we caught up to her.

"Elyse," we said in unison.

She turned toward us.

"Mom?" It came out a question, but I already knew the answer.

She clasped her hands near her chest. "My girls," she said. "Ellen and Stella."

"What are you doing here?" Stella asked in a neutral voice.

"I heard about your father, and I—I had to come." She looked at me, then at Stella. "I hope you don't mind."

People were starting to trickle out of the room now. I grabbed Elyse's forearm and pulled her into the next room. Stella followed and shut the door behind us.

"I can't believe you're here," I told her.

"We were just at your park," Stella said, at the same time.

"We heard you speak," I said.

"We just found you," said Stella.

Elyse laughed softly. "I didn't know I was lost."

"What?" Stella and I said together. We looked at each other, then back at Elyse.

"What do you mean, you didn't know you were lost?" Stella asked. "You let us think you'd died."

"You clearly didn't want us to look for you," I said.

Elyse paled. "You thought I had died?" She whispered. "Oh, no." She shook her head. "Oh, no no no." She paused. "I left a note. Didn't you find my note? Didn't your father find it?"

We answered with blank stares.

"I didn't want to leave you." She held one hand up to her mouth as if to suppress the impact her words might have on us. "Before I met Fossil, I was married to a horrible man who made me—do horrible things—and I escaped." She spoke a little faster and her voice was gaining strength. "I climbed out of a restaurant bathroom window and hid in a ditch until after sunset, then I hitchhiked a few hundred miles until I arrived in Iron Falls, and met your dad."

Stella's face looked as shocked as I felt.

"I never thought he'd try to find me, but he did." She paused, as if reliving that moment. "He found me, and he threatened to abuse both of you if I didn't go with him immediately." A tear rolled down her face, gathering speed as it crested her cheekbone. "I hated him. I hated what he made me do." She took a deep breath and let it out slowly. "The worst thing he did was make me leave you girls. But there was no way I could take you. I knew you'd be safe here, and I would do anything to ensure you were safe."

Muted conversations drifted past the door.

"A few years later, I escaped again. This time, from a gas station bathroom. It's funny," she said, looking unamused, "I've had to start over so many times, and twice, a bathroom escape was involved." She shook her head.

"We thought you left us," said Stella.

"We thought you died," I said at the same time.

"We thought you died, and left us," said Stella.

"But your—Fossil. I wrote him a note! I left it in the jewelry box. I didn't tell him the whole truth, of course." She shook her head. "I couldn't imagine telling him what I'd escaped. But I told him—in the note—to tell you girls about me, and to tell you I hoped to see you again one day. I told him to tell you I loved you." She folded her arms and clutched her elbows. "I thought you didn't want to see me." She sniffed, wiped a tear. "All these years, I thought you didn't want to see me."

Stella took a step toward her and gathered her into a hug. After a moment, they beckoned me and I joined in.

"This time," Elyse whispered, clearly unwilling to break up our hug, "I can start over because I want to, not because I have to. I've missed you girls so."

We stood there like that, a column of grief, until everyone had left the funeral home and Mick found us by opening random doors.

Althea: Six months AF*

*After Fossil

Courtney is establishing herself as a premiere cyber forensic technician. She accepted a second case a few days ago, and she deputized me to be her right-hand sleuth. Mom hired us to locate her friend Imogene Whitaker, formerly known as Madge, short for imagine, an early childhood mispronunciation of her name. The only clues we have so far are the convoluted nickname and her street address in 1993.

I'm confident in our abilities to locate Madge, judging from our stellar success with our previous case. So far, we have a 100% success rate.

The side effects of solving our first case continue to surprise and comfort me. I don't feel like an unfinished sentence anymore—I have two halves, and you can barely see the seam or tell which half is the new half and which is the old. My two halves fit together like puzzle pieces.

My favorite thing to say is "I'm going to my Dad's". And it's true! I'm really going there, right now, on the bus, in broad daylight, and this is my third trip. When we went back to Madison a few weeks after my escapade, as Mom calls it, Mom and Dad (doesn't that sound great?) agreed that I can visit every month. Mom went with me the first time, and I've been going by myself ever since. To my dad's.

I don't have a list of tolerations anymore—now I just tolerate things without writing them down. It's much easier. I make lists of things to do with my brothers, things to do with my dad and step-mom, and things to do with my mom, because she's still my fave and I don't want her to forget it.

Malcolm will be disappointed when he finds out I'm not going to Harvard.

It's too far away from my dad.

Elle: Six months AF*

*After Fossil

Joel knocked on the open door as he walked in. "It smells great in here."

"Thanks! We're having lasagne. I modified my recipe when I stopped eating meat years ago, but it's still quite popular with carnivores."

Joel laughed at this and pulled a bouquet of tulips and a bottle of wine from the bag he carried. "These are for you, and this is for us. Do you have a vase and a corkscrew?"

"They're lovely—tulips are my favorite flowers. Thank you." I reached above the sink to grab a crystal vase, and directed Joel to the drawer containing the corkscrew.

We worked in silence for a few minutes—I finished assembling the dressing and tossing the salad, and he opened the wine so it could breathe for a few minutes before I served dinner. My mood matched the weather today: sunny with a light breeze. My ring finger felt naked and exposed.

"Where's Althea? I thought she'd be joining us." Joel looked at me and mimed pouring the wine into a glass.

I handed him two glasses. "She's at her dad's."

His head snapped up. "Her dad's? I thought—wait a minute, where's your ring?"

I paused. "Instead of Althea, my mom will be joining us for dinner. She's in town for the weekend."

"Your—what?" He shook his head. "I think I missed something." He pulled out a chair for me, so I could sit across the table from him. "Start at the beginning. Tell me everything. And don't forget to tell me about the ring."

And I did. I told him everything, or at least my side of everything. My truth. I told him I no longer wished for a DeLorean full of plutonium, that I'd finally made peace with my past and present.

I told him the ring was nestled safely in a jewelry box, and I no longer felt the need to wear it.

Joel said he'd be my plutonium.

I might let him.

Acknowledgements

This book began with a vague impression of friendship between a young girl and an elderly man. The story underwent several major changes and rewrites, two deep edits, and countless iterations before it assumed its final shape. This book took the longest for me to write, and it was the most difficult story for me to write, compared to my other works thus far. It would not exist if it weren't for the help I received along the way.

My Alpha Readers, Jen Postula and Angela Leonard, provided much needed encouragement and advice on my first draft. Thank you for helping me smooth out the roughest phrases, and for recognizing the potential in the collection of looseleaf paper you read so many months ago.

Thank you, Cathy Yardley, for your kind words and encouragement, and for helping me to decide Elyse's fate (which has since been changed again).

My faithful editor, Teresa Crumpton, once again (twice, actually) solved some of the major problems and challenged me to define Ellen's story. Thank you, Teresa, for your patience and tact. Hearing criticism is never easy but Teresa delivers it with aplomb.

I'm also grateful to my family—my mom, my sister, and my daughters—for listening to my ruminations about Ellen and Stella and Althea throughout this process, and helping me brainstorm and plot, and encouraging me to write.

This is the first book I've written that has a Beta Readers Launch Team, and I thank all of my Beta Readers for the valuable feedback and comments. There are countless others (okay, about seven) who always ask me how my writing is going, and when my next book will be out. Thank you for that—these comments motivate me to run to my laptop and type until my fingers go numb.

About the Author

Jan Stafford Kellis was born reading and started writing soon thereafter. Words continue to fascinate her, and she reads and writes every day. She lives in the eastern end (the best end) of Michigan's Upper Peninsula, where the living is easy and the inspiration is plentiful.

Jan read her way through school, hastening to finish schoolwork so she could read. She carried a book with her everywhere she went, and this practice continues today. If you happen to see Jan in line at a store or stopped at a road construction site, chances are she's reading, hoping the delay lasts until the end of the chapter.

When Jan isn't reading or writing, she's probably visiting her daughters or her sister, or sewing, quilting, crocheting, traveling, marathon shopping or luxury camping. She hasn't been bored since 1974, when she learned how to read.

Bookstores are her favorite attractions and are always part of her travel itineraries.

For the latest updates, or to book an appearance, please visit www.jankellis.com.

Other Books by Jan Stafford Kellis

Bookworms Anonymous, Volume I

The true tale of a non-traditional book club in De Tour Village, located in Michigan's Upper Peninsula. This book provides a bookworm's eye view of book club meetings (they're never called parties!) and includes book reviews, book handling commandments, recipes and a guide for beginning your own chapter of Bookworms Anonymous.

Bookworms Anonymous, Volume II

The Worms are gathered again! *Bookworms Anonymous Volume II* contains many of the same things found in Volume I: reading group meetings, anecdotes, book reviews and recipes.

"A delightful read for any book lover, Bookworms Anonymous II is packed with great reading recommendations and insightful conversation from seven savvy readers. Book club-friendly recipes are a delicious bonus! Now, I'm off to the bookstore..." - Kathleen Flinn, author of *The Sharper Your Knife, the Less You Cry* and *The Kitchen Counter Cooking School*

"A warm celebration of two of life's most vital ingredients--books and friendships." - Ellen Airgood, author of *South of Superior* and *Prairie Evers*

"A love letter to reading, beautifully rendered, and with all the warmth and fun and closeness of your favorite book club on that perfect meeting night." - Robert Kurson, author of *Shadow Divers* and *Crashing Through*

The Word That You Heard

Enid Forrester hates her name and her hair. On the first day of summer in 1980 she can almost see the wonderfully empty expanse of time stretching before her. Enid comes of age in Michigan's Upper Peninsula, where there isn't much to do in the summer or any other time of year for a twelve-year-old girl. Her summer education includes listening to the "drunken pontificators" lecture in the coffee shop about what not to do as she joins her dad at the local table for their morning refueling. Enid learns life can't be distilled into mere words and small towns sometimes offer the widest view of humanity.

A Pocketful of Light

Italy has it all and she's willing to share. Explore the world's original tourist destination through this true story told like a novel. The book features the Fibonacci Sequence, a few non-painful history lessons and some funky Italian phrases as well as the friendly recounting of two travelers exploring the second greatest country in the world.

Superior Sacrifices

This is the story of Mitch and Marcia: twins, best friends and local celebrities in the small town of Iron Falls, Michigan. Mitch's superhuman dedication to his detective job and Marcia's near-obsessive focus on her family and bookstore business appear ordinary until the secret they've shared for three and a half decades threatens to surface.

All books are available in fine book stores and www.amazon.com.

Would you like a FREE copy of the
Bookworms Anonymous Cookbooklet?
Subscribe to Jan's email list at www.jankellis.com, and get your free copy!

Made in the USA
Charleston, SC
07 July 2016